Howard Overing Sturgis

Tim

To her for whose entertainment it was originally written,
this story belongs as of right.
On the shrine of her deathless memory
I lay my little book.

Howard Overing Sturgis

Gay Classics Series

Tim

By

Howard Overing Sturgis

Author of "All That Was Possible"
and "Belchamber"

"Thy love to me was wonderful,
passing the love of women."

MONDIAL

Mondial
New York

Gay Classics Series

Howard Overing Sturgis: Tim
(1891)

Copyright © 2009 Mondial
(for this print edition of "Tim")
Editor (2009): Andrew Moore

Cover image © Uday K. Dhar

ISBN 978-1-59569-130-9
Library of Congress Control Number: 2009922172

www.mondialbooks.com

CHAPTER I

And he wandered away and away
With Nature the dear old nurse,
Who sang to him, night and day,
The rhymes of the universe.

Longfellow's *Fiftieth Birthday of Agassis.*

Tim's real name was not Tim: so much is certain. What it was, I have never inquired. The nickname had been bestowed on him so early in life that the memory of such men and women as knew him ran not to the contrary. Tim was Tim by immemorial custom; even his father, who had little reverence for established usages, never thought of altering this one, and, as one name is as good as another, we too will call him by the only one by which he was ever known.

Tim was a slightly-made, lean, brown child, but without the pretty colour brown children usually have. He had such regular little features and such a pale little face that he might almost have been called faded, had he ever looked otherwise. Mrs. Quitchett had pronounced him to be 'the thinnest and lightest baby ever she see,' when he was transferred to her care from that of the monthly nurse, in which opinion she was supported by that lady, who might be said to be an authority on such matters. Possibly she too might throw some light on the question of how he came by that prebaptismal nickname of his, for she alone had had much to do with him previous to the day when he had been carried, a poor little skinny Christian-elect, to be received into the pale of the Church.

That event was seven years into the past at the time I write of, and Tim, despite his puny appearance, having struggled through the usual maladies of childhood, and cut several of his second teeth, was living in an old house in one of the western counties of England.

The Stoke Ashton manor-house, of which the most modern rooms dated from the days of Elizabeth, had been the home of the Darley family through ages of unbroken descent, until a part of it having been destroyed by fire in the year of our Lord 1780, the then existing Darley had built the big house up in the park, and called it Darley Court. Thenceforward for the next seventy years or so, what was left of the manor-house became the abode of widowed mothers, spinster sisters, or married sons, until the day when, no such relative laying claim to it at the moment, old Squire Darley let it to Tim's parents.

The first seven years of the child's life in the queer old house could not well have been less eventful. He was happy enough in the company of Mrs. Quitchett and his old setter Bess, partly perhaps from never having known any other.

'His father,' nurse told him, 'was in India.'

'Where was that?' asked Tim.

'Oh! a long way off.'

'Farther than Granthurst?'

'Yes, much farther.'

The schoolmaster, who came and gave him a lesson now and then, showed him India on the map, but he was not much the wiser. His mother, Mrs. Quitchett never mentioned, and as she never introduced the subject, he asked no questions, having the habit of deferring to her in all matters, and her rule, though absolute, was not a hard one. There was only one point on which he ever questioned her authority: in his determination on no account to wear a hat, he was adamant. We all have our idiosyncrasies, and this was Tim's. On Sundays alone could he be prevailed upon to allow a small round covering of mixed straw to be stuck on the extreme back of his head, when Mrs. Quitchett took him to church in his best clothes. At first, when he was very little, his picture-book used to be taken with him; but when he was considered to have reached an age at which the rector's discourses would be of service to him, this indulgence was withdrawn, and he found thenceforward his principal entertainment in the painted window just opposite his seat. It had been put up in memory of some dead child, and the subject had a great fascination for Tim, who used to call it 'his' window. It represented a long stretch of quiet upland, arched by a twilight sky paling into a streak of soft light where it disappeared on the distant horizon; walking across the green came the tender gracious figure of the good shepherd bearing a lamb in his loving arms. Tim knew just such a bit of down where the lambs played, and could almost fancy sometimes that he saw the figure coming towards him from out of the sunset. The whole picture was subdued in colouring, and set for sharp contrast in a frame of tall lilies and jubilant golden-haired angels. Not less bright was the head of the Squire's little grandson, who sometimes knelt in the big Court pew hard by, where, almost hidden from the rest of the church, old Mr. Darley persisted in attending worship, to the scandal of his daughter Miss Kate, who inclined to High Church, and to whom tall family pews which turned their backs on the altar were an abomination.

Thus once a week did Tim conform to laws social and religious, but the other six days saw him scudding bareheaded over the fields, searching for flowers along the hedgerows, or, tired at last with his wanderings, sitting by the side of some little brook nursing his knees, and singing low to himself little quaint snatches of song culled here and there from old books, and set to the nursery tunes Mrs. Quitchett hummed to him, or to others picked up, Heaven knows where,— perhaps from the birds.

No place came amiss to Tim as a resting-place except a chair; he would sit on the soft green grass, in a tree, on a stile, a table, a window-sill,—anywhere but on those articles of furniture which custom has set aside for the purpose. In the winter he and Bess curled themselves up in the shaggy bearskin rug before the fire and fell asleep; in the summer he sat in the patches of sun on the carpet, and told Bess stories from the *Arabian Nights*, of which he had discovered a copy with pictures in the old library. The fairy Pari-banou unlocked the wonders of her palace for that patient hound; Prince Firouz Shah flew by on the enchanted horse, Morgiana whirled in her dance, and Gulnaré rose from the sea to be the bride of the Persian king; only the story of the lady who whipped the little dogs Tim never related, out of consideration for his companion's feelings.

Such was Tim's life: reading to a dog, singing to the streams, having fellowship with birds and flowers, in a strange world of his own creation, hatless, lean, brown, and happy. The hours slipped softly by him without his noting their passing. He knew when it was Sunday, was glad when it was fine, not sorry when it rained, full of strange dreams and fancies, companionless yet not alone, for nature was with him. And so Tim grew to be eight years old.

One day the postman brought Mrs. Quitchett a letter which had come all the way from India,— and a long way it was in those days when no Suez Canal existed to shorten the journey. The letter had no beginning, because Tim's father, who had written it, was a man who never quite knew how to begin his letters to an old nurse. To say 'Dear Mrs. Quitchett' seemed to imply undue familiarity. 'Madam' was altogether out of the question. 'Mrs. Quitchett' sounded harsh and dictatorial, which he had no wish to be, and to write a long letter in the third person would have been a needless exertion. So the letter came to the point at once, without preliminary compliment.

'You will perhaps be surprised to hear,' it said, in neat upstrokes and downstrokes and beautifully straight lines, 'that I intend coming home for good. My doctor strongly advises my leaving India, and I am the more inclined to consent that I am very desirous of seeing my son, to whom I am of opinion that the personal care of a father may be of more service during such time as I am spared to him, than a somewhat larger fortune at my death.'

Nurse Quitchett glanced over her venerable spectacles at Tim, who was lying asleep on the window-seat, with his arm round the neck of the faithful Bess, but returned without making any remark to her reading.

'You will have the goodness to acquaint my son with my change of plans. I shall probably reach home by about October, and shall hope to find my boy ready to give me a welcome. I am afraid his education must have been rather neglected, but he is young yet, and that deficiency may easily be supplied; while I am sure that in your hands his health at least must have been well looked after. I have always disapproved of the self-ishness of some Indian parents who, keeping their children with them in an unhealthy climate for their own gratification, injure their health per-haps for life. I hope to be repaid for my six years' separation from my only child by finding a true, sturdy little pink-and-white Briton waiting to greet me on my return. With my best thanks for your care of the boy and the regular reports you have sent me of him, believe me, truly yours,

'*William Ebbesley.*'

Mrs. Quitchett put down the letter, took off her glasses, which were somehow quite wet, and looked again, not without apprehension, at the sleeping boy. In vain she tried to make any of the epithets used in the let-ter fit the child before her: he was as unlike the picture of the true, sturdy little pink-and-white Briton, on which his father's fancy dwelt so fondly, as one boy could be unlike another.

William Ebbesley, observing that Anglo-Indian babies were as a rule small and sallow, had concluded, with defective logic, that his child, not being brought up in India, would be neither the one nor the other. He had thought of this imaginary child of his, until, Prometheus-like, he had given life to the figure he had himself created; and had any one cared to inquire what the boy was like, would unhesitatingly have described him. Nowadays his illusions would be rudely dispelled by photography; but when Tim was a child, the art was also in its infancy, and it had not become the fashion to have babies photographed once a year. On one occasion, when Tim was three years old, Mrs. Quitchett had set up his hair in a sort of crest and carried him to a neighbouring town to be photo-graphed, but the child could not be got to sit still, and ended by a flood of tears, so that the little card which finally went to Mr. Ebbesley was hardly satisfactory as a likeness. Mrs. Quitchett herself confessed as much, and the father was quite indignant at this libel on his child. It never even oc-curred to him that the photograph, bad as it was, had at least been taken from the real boy, and as such might be nearer the truth than the portrait his fancy had painted.

Writing not being a strong point of Mrs. Quitchett's, her epistolary style was remarkable chiefly for its terseness, and she would as soon have thought of writing a novel at once as of launching into any description of Tim's appearance, beyond such casual expressions of admiration as nurses use of their bantlings, and which are not meant to be taken literally.

After a while Tim stirred uneasily, and Bess, roused into semi-consciousness by his change of position, put up her cold nose and touched his cheek. The boy woke with a start and sat up, to find the eyes of his old nurse fixed on him with an expression he had never seen in them before; it was gone as soon as she saw that he was awake, but not before he had remarked it, and springing quickly to her he asked, 'Why do you look at me like that? What have you got there?'

The second question happily furnishing nurse with an excuse for evading the first, which she would have been puzzled how to answer, 'It's a letter from your papa,' she said, 'and I've got a surprise for you; what do you think is going to happen?'

'He's coming home,' replied Tim quietly, as if he had known it all along.

'Law bless the boy!' called out Mrs. Quitchett. 'Whoever could have told you? But there! nobody could, for I've just this minute finished reading the letter, and it's not been out of my hand.'

Tim nodded sagaciously: 'I dreamed it,' he said, as he walked off into the garden, leaving his nurse in that condition which she would herself have described as a capability of being knocked down with a feather.

'Well, of all the out-of-the-way odd children ever I see!' she ejaculated under her breath; and then the father's picture of the little Briton recurred to her so pathetically comic in its contrast to facts, that she could not help smiling, though the tears followed close after, as she thought, 'He'll come between me and my boy; well, I ought to ha' known how it would be.'

But though the old nurse might shed a few tears in private, and to Tim the words 'My father is coming' conveyed, it is true, some misty sense of approaching change, the letter and its contents left no perceptible mark on the inhabitants of the manor-house. Mrs. Quitchett could not spare much time to speculation, and her charge had not contracted the habit of looking ahead; what difference his father's home-coming would make in his life he knew not, and scarcely cared to imagine.

The summer passed away in no respect unlike those other five or six he could remember. The roses bloomed and paled and fell; the birds built their nests, laid their eggs, hatched and reared their young, all in due order; the cornfields passed through all their accustomed phases; July succeeded to June, August to July, September to August, and 'Nature the dear old nurse' led this youngest of her nurslings through the peaceful hot months, unsuspicious of those that were to follow.

The first touch of autumn saddened our Tim; the waving fields of golden grain, with their wind-rippled orange shadows, had lent a thrill of happiness to a little soul alive to all such influences, and now that the meek, stately ears had bowed their heads to the sickle, he missed their presence, and sorrowed over the stubble.

This month, too, the guns were popping all over the country-side, and Tim hated guns for two reasons — first, because they startled the quiet of his usual rambles, giving a sense of insecurity even to the quietest fields; and secondly, because each report that made the child jump and tremble, meant the death or wounding of a bird; and that was keen grief to him.

CHAPTER II

. . . and the sweet smell of the fields
Past, and the sunshine came along with him.

Tennyson's *Pelleas and Ettarre.*

One day a party of gentlemen set out from Darley Court to shoot partridges. Old Squire Darley was an open-handed man, and loved his kind well enough to be glad to fill his house with them two or three times a year; but better than all else in the world did he love his grandson Carol, and Carol was worth loving. A brighter, truer, more boyish boy than Carol Darley did not exist in all England; he was straight as a little dart, had never had a day's illness in his life, and was blessed, in addition to an excellent temper and tearing spirits, with a frame slight as yet, but well knit and vigorous, a broad frank face, a joyous mouth, a bright colour, a shock of golden curls, and two such honest kindly blue eyes, that you might draw gladness from them like water from a well. And the old man would have loved him had he come to him with none of these claims for affection, for was he not the point in which all his hopes and cares centred, the sole survivor of his house, the child of his dead son? The child had come to the two old people like a message straight from heaven, in their heaviest grief. The first reawakening to life after their crushing loss was the discovery that the little lips had been taught to call the old place 'home.'

Carol was thirteen on this particular morning, and to-day, in fulfilment of a promise of long standing, his grandfather had promoted him from trotting about after the shooters, as he had hitherto done, to carrying a gun of his own. Earth seemed to have nothing more to offer as he strutted along in the clear September sunshine, bravely brushing last night's raindrops from the heavy turnip-tops with his sturdy legs; already he foresaw himself the best shot in the county, as his father had been before him. To be sure, he had not shot anything as yet, and the little gun kicked rather and hurt his shoulder, but such trifles as these were powerless to dash his joy; only he did hope he should shoot something before he had to go home.

'That's a fine boy of yours, Darley,' said one of the gentlemen; 'he steps out well. Shall you send him into the army?'

The Squire swelled with honest pride as his eye fell on the boy. 'Well, I hardly know yet,' he answered; 'it seems a good soldier wasted, and yet

I have always set my heart on his making a figure in the county— going into Parliament, and all that; it wouldn't be the first time a member had come from Darley. I used to hope his father—but there, we never know what is best for us,' added the old man hastily. Mr. Darley felt quite sorry that he could not bestow Carol on all the careers open to him; he was so eminently qualified to adorn whichever might finally be selected for honour, that it was difficult to make a wise choice. The army was a gentlemanly calling, but Mrs. Darley would not hear of that for a moment. 'Suppose there should be a war,' she said. Sometimes the Squire had leanings towards the Woolsack, or if Miss Kate suggested the Church, he had visions of Carol in lawn sleeves crowning sovereigns and christening royal infants; but on the whole, though with a sense that he was defrauding all the professions, he felt that the important post of Squire of Darley was the one for which his treasure was pre-eminently fitted; and there at least I think he was right. The object of all this anxious thought was not as yet gone to Eton, which was to be the next step on his road to greatness, where he would wear a round jacket, and perhaps be whipped; but if the road we look along be straight, the eye does not accurately measure the distance.

The party of shooters were walking along a turnip-field bordered on one side by a hazel coppice, when the dogs put up a covey of six birds a little in front of them. Two got away, two fell, and the remaining two flew for the coppice, on the side on which Carol was walking.

'Now then, sir,' cried his grandfather, 'the birds are waiting for you; winged, by Jove! no, missed. You little goose! Bless my soul, what was that?'

'That' was a sort of cry which proceeded from the coppice into which most of Carol's charge had gone, and quite unlike any note of partridge or other bird. The boy's bright colour faded from his cheeks, and he put down his gun as though by impulse, but could not move; he stood wide-eyed, staring at the tangle of slender hazel rods from which the sound had come. Some of the party, however, knowing that these accidents were not of a fatal kind, parted the branches and disclosed to view a small figure habited in an old holland blouse, stretched among the sticks and dry leaves which strewed the ground. The child lay quite still, and on nearer approach proved to have fainted. Carol now came near, steadying himself by his grandfather's kind hand.

'Is he dead?' he asked in a whisper, all the horror of having killed his fellow-boy surging over his bright young heart like a drowning wave.

'Dead! no, no, no,' answered the Colonel good-naturedly (he who had asked whether Carol was to be put into the army); 'he's been grazed, nothing more. It's the fright that made the poor child faint; any doctor will pick out the shot in five minutes, and to-morrow he'll be trotting about again.'

Carol said nothing, but big tears of thankfulness swelled up in his bonnie blue eyes, and the Squire felt the boy's grasp tighten in his. He had to turn away himself (tears are so infectious), and to adopt a jovially bustling manner, as he asked the keeper if he knew whose child this was.

'If you please, sir,' said the man, 'it's the little gentleman as lives in the old manor-house along of the old lady.'

'Dear, dear—dear, dear! take him home, some one; I will send down this evening and inquire. Anything that is wanted, if they will only let us know, we will be too happy; remember to say that; be sure you say we shall be so glad to send anything.'

Here a grateful pressure from the little hand in his caused him to look at his grandson. The boy was still white, and the old man took alarm at once. 'Why, Carol—boy, come home, come home; it's nothing, sir; didn't you hear what the Colonel said? All right to-morrow,' and he departed, dragging his unwilling grandson after him, unheeding his entreaties to be allowed to accompany those of the party who undertook, guided by the keeper, to convey our wounded hero to the experienced care of Mrs. Quitchett, for whom, now that he was come to himself, he had begun in a feeble way to ask.

That lady considered it due to herself to betray no emotion in the presence of 'the gentlemen' further than a violent pull at a wandering string of her cap, which caused that erection to assume a sidelong position, and imparted to her a certain wildness of appearance, strangely at variance with the studied impassiveness of her bearing.

There was something distrustful, even defiant, in her manner, thinly disguised under an assumption of extreme deference, as she 'thanked them for the trouble they had been at, and sent her duty to Mr. Darley; but they had all that they wanted, she thanked him. Then, when she had bowed them out, paying but scant attention to expressions of interest and concern, she bundled off the garden-boy post-haste for the doctor, and undressed her charge and got him to bed with wonderful celerity.

When the doctor came he made light of her anxiety, assuring her the boy was hardly scratched, picked out the shot, at which Tim winced, and departed, promising to look in in the morning.

After the tumult comes peace, and in the course of the long, drowsy afternoon, when his kind nurse brought her work to sit by him, Tim narrated the events of the morning in his own fashion.

'You know I hate the guns,' he began, 'and I'd gone up by the hazel coppice above Beech Farm, because I thought I should be out of the way of them, and I was sitting in there; it's one of my houses, you know, — in the dining-room I was. We were having dinner — make-believe dinner, you know — I and the squirrel — only I had to make-believe the squirrel too, because he wouldn't come near enough — I suppose he thought I should hurt him, but he needn't have thought that, need he? Well, just then I heard voices in the field outside, and there were the dogs quite close. I stayed quiet, for I thought they would go by; but there came a sound of wings, and quick, one after the other, two shots — bang, bang, and I jumped up to run; but there were shouts, and then another shot, and I felt I was hit, and fell down, for I thought I was killed; and I don't remember much more till I got back here.'

So far all was coherent enough, a rare virtue in Tim's account of events, in which, as a rule, his fancy made such havoc of mere prose facts, that it was hard to distinguish what he only thought had happened from what had actually taken place. But after a minute or two of silence he added —

'And, nurse, do you know, I think there was an angel there.'

'Lor' bless the child!' thought Mrs. Quitchett; 'now he's off, I suppose.'

'It was in the part I don't much remember,' Tim went on; 'it was only the face. I didn't notice it at the time, but I can remember it now quite plain. It had golden hair, where the sun shone on it, like the angels in my window in church, and big blue eyes. I remember it now, though I did not notice it then, which is odd, nurse, isn't it?'

'There, there,' said Mrs. Quitchett hastily, 'that'll do; you've talked as much as is good for you, and more too; maybe you did see one. Now you just lie quiet and go to sleep.' And Tim obeyed and went to sleep; and in the evening when the groom from the Court came 'to enquire,' a most satisfactory account of his condition was returned to the Darleys, which comforted Carol not a little.

That youth, as a gentleman who went out shooting and dined late, considered himself as formed, and spoke of the infantile brown holland Tim as 'poor child' with lofty compassion. Now that all was going well, he forgot his fright, and bragged quite grandly about the day's sport to the lady next him at dinner. 'Thirty brace and a few rabbits to six guns; not a bad bag, was it, for a half day?'

'And how much of it did *you* shoot?' asked his neighbour tartly, who was too young herself to tolerate the boy's youthful boasting; damsels of eighteen do not like a spoilt boy about the house. Carol blushed a fine pink, and then burst out laughing at his own discomfiture.

'Don't you know,' said his friend the Colonel, who sat on the other side of Miss, 'that you must never ask a man that question? You ask what the bag was, and politely take it for granted that each of us contributed his fair share. Our friend there, who, with the modesty of all truly great men, blushes at the record of his own deeds, can't tell you in my presence how he had to cover my deficiencies; besides,' he added, with a knowing look at poor Carol, which deepened the glow on the lad's face, 'bringing down a very remarkable head of large game, the like of which, I will undertake to say, is not in any bag in the county.'

Carol, you may be sure, sat over his wine with the other gentlemen, feeling that that was due to himself, though his thoughts wandered continually to some mysterious telegraphic tackle in one of the trees on the lawn, the condition of which he was burning to inspect, while he busied himself with collecting various provisions from the dishes nearest to him, to be conveyed, by and by, to a squirrel, his prisoner and dependant. The Squire always liked to have the boy near himself, and used to say, 'We are all the better, I take it, for having to be a little careful what we say.' The conversation did not interest the lad for the most part, being mainly political (for Mr. Darley was a keen politician); but presently his attention was attracted by hearing the Colonel talking of the event of the morning. 'That was a strange little mortal that got hurt to-day,' he was saying. To which the Squire, who was a little deaf, answered promptly, 'Ah! thank you; the groom came back just before dinner. The doctor says it was nothing. Going on as well as possible, thank God; but it might have been a nasty thing.'

'I am glad he's all right, poor child. Whose child, by the way, did you say he was? Surely not the old cat's in the Egyptian headgear.'

'Ah! 'pon my life, it's a sad story. I remember their first coming down here, nine or ten years ago it must be. They took the old manor-house, — it should have been my poor dear Harry's, but his wife couldn't bear the place; but there, she's gone, poor woman, and it's all over now. What was I saying? Ah! the little boy. Yes. Ebbesley their name was. He must have been going on for forty; looked older, a good deal older, than his wife; a very handsome woman I recollect. He had made money in India; men get on young there — bar, civil service, I don't know what. He's gone back there now; been there ever since, . . .' and here the old gentleman, observing Master Carol's blue eyes very big and fixed on him, mumbled something to his friend that had Latin words in it; Carol heard *debetur pueris*, but did not know what they meant.

'And the child you saw to-day was their son,' the Squire went on; 'he was born soon after they came here.'

'And does he live there all by himself, with that old woman?'

'I believe he must. The old woman must be his nurse; I never thought of him much till to-day. Lord knows how he's got educated, or if he ever has. He must have had a dull childhood; perhaps I ought to have seen after him, but we were never over intimate with the parents. My wife didn't take to Mrs. Ebbesley from the first: you see our Kate was a young girl then, and we had to be careful for her, you know. But the poor little boy must be very lonely. Will you have some more wine? No? Then we'll have our coffee with the ladies.'

'My dear,' said Mrs. Darley to her husband, as he came in last of the black coats from the dining-room, 'didn't you say that Carol turned quite white when he heard that little boy scream?'

'As white as your cap, ma'am.'

'There,' said Mrs. Darley triumphantly to her daughter, 'and the doctor has told me so often that after a sudden shock any one ought always to take a little dose.'

Miss Kate, a kind-hearted but stern lady of two-and-thirty, who loved her nephew dearly, but was forced to act as a sort of permanent drag on her parents' exuberant affection, protested vainly that the boy looked as well as she had ever seen him. When he went to bed his grandmother drew him mysteriously into her dressing-room, and presented him with a small round globule, and directions for use. She would have been less pleased, I fear, with his improved appearance next morning had she seen him, on reaching his apartment, pound the medicine up fine, and cautiously scatter the dust out of the window, where, we will hope, some dyspeptic sparrow was benefited by it, for no one else ever was. It is a sad fact that a great part of the contents of the good old lady's medicine-chest was disposed of in this fashion.

At Carol's age, however, a good night will repair most nervous shocks without artificial aids, and he was up early next morning, and down in the garden as soon as breakfast was over. The art of coaxing was an open book to Carol, and he attacked the old Scotch gardener, — with whom, as with every one else, he was a prime favourite, — in his most fascinating manner. After much judiciously administered sympathy for his friend's pet grievances, 'Please, I want a bunch of grapes.' he said presently.

'I mayna let ye have the greeps, Masterrr Carrel.'

'Oh but, M'Allan, they're not for me; they are for some one who is ill. I must really have a bunch, please. I'm sure grandpapa wouldn't mind, — and some leaves, please, to put in this basket.'

Of course he had his way in the end, and set off with his booty in the direction of the manor-house, as hard as his legs would carry him.

Mrs. Quitchett saw him coming as she stood in the doorway, shading her spectacles with her hand, looking out for the doctor. Did she forecast in her mind some part of what should follow on this visit? She was certainly far from guessing the whole of it.

Tim had passed a rather restless night, full of short broken dreams, in all of which, the 'angel' of his adventure had played a prominent part. Now that he was up and dressed, he still felt tired, and was lying on his favourite window-seat looking out at the already changing trees. He heard the door open but did not turn his head, till a strange voice, young and clear, quite unlike the doctor's, which he had expected, said, with a pretty hesitation, 'I have brought you some grapes; I hope you are all right this morning; I . . .' and there stopped, for Tim had started up and was sitting staring, with his heart in his eyes. There within a few feet of him was the face he had seen in his dreams, the face of his 'angel.' It seemed quite natural to him to hold out his arms; God had sent his angel to comfort him. Carol was not fond of kissing, and had all a boy's horror of being seen to perform that operation, but he could not resist the mute appeal of those outstretched arms, though he did not know what prompted it. He went forward half frank and half embarrassed, and stooping down, kissed Tim's poor little pale face. Then Mrs. Quitchett said, 'Here's young Master Darley has brought you some grapes,' and Tim bounced back to earth out of his dreamland, and was taken very shy, scarce finding words to say 'Thank you.'

CHAPTER III

... for Enoch seem'd to them
Uncertain as a vision or a dream,
Faint as a figure seen in early dawn
Down at the far end of an avenue,
Going we know not where. . . .

Tennyson's *Enoch Arden.*

Carol did not stay long, but promised to come soon again, which left Tim in a quiver of excitement, and thinking him the kindest, the handsomest, the most brilliant person he had ever seen. It is odd that these two boys should have lived so near one another so long without becoming acquainted; but it must be remembered that Tim's life had been one of cloistral seclusion. If he had been dimly conscious at times that people spoke of the Squire's grandson, he had paid as little attention to that as to other things that they said. Since Darley had been his home, Carol had been much away at school, and in his holidays, had noticed Tim, if he saw him, as he noticed any other child about the village, without attaching any particular identity to him, for it is fair to acknowledge that there was nothing remarkable in Tim's appearance shrinking into the hedge with his burden of wildflowers, as the other boy flashed by on his pony. But now that the child was weak and ill, and, above all, reduced to that condition by an act of his, all Carol's generous young soul was stirred in his behalf; and the bunch of grapes was the first result of this blind instinct of obligation to protect and cherish the innocent victim of his bow and spear. You may fancy if the old people at the Court rejoiced over this touching and beautiful action of their darling when they came to hear of it.

'What a dear good boy that is, upon my soul!' said the Squire, squeezing his old wife's hand; and she, with a tear in her eye, answered, 'We've great cause to be thankful, Hugh! The Lord has taken away, but He's given again; it's like having Harry back.' And they shook their kind old heads, recalling other instances of singular goodness in Carol, and traits of likeness to his father. Harry had given his sixpence to the blind beggar, and Carol had saved up his pennies to buy a crutch for the lame boy at the shoemaker's. Once the Squire had met his grandson assisting a certain crone, of great age and most forbidding aspect, to carry a load of faggots she had been collecting in the Court woods for her wretched little fire. This goody was, I regret to say, a most abandoned old woman, and a sworn enemy of Mrs. Darley; refusing point-blank to attend church, and strongly suspected of foxlike visits to the good lady's hen-roost. Moreover, the Squire was very particular about the sanctity of the timber in his woods. But on this occasion he not only pardoned the trespasser, but gave her permission to boil her skinny pot over his sticks for the future; until some fresh outrage on her part put her once more without the pale of society. So the objects of Carol's kindness shone with a borrowed light, and were dear to his relatives as so many proofs of the extraordinary amiability of the lad's disposition.

Tim became an object of great interest to the Darleys: Miss Kate came to see him, and Mrs. Darley, bringing jelly and other good things, such as soft fussy old ladies love to take to sick folk. And the Squire came himself, saying that 'Upon his word, Tim was a very nice little fellow, and when he got better must come to see them at the Court.' a prospect that alarmed him not a little. And they had plenty of chances of visiting the child, for Tim was ill longer than could have been expected. One day, when the doctor had seen him, he stopped as he left the house and said to Mrs. Quitchett, 'You must take care of this little man, nurse; he is by temperament an excitable child. So slight a scratch as he got would have had no effect on most boys, but the shock has evidently told on him; he is a little feverish and must be kept quiet.'

Then he paused a little, pulling at the clematis round the porch, as though weighing the desirability of saying more, decided to do so, and added with just a shade more impressiveness in his voice —

'Things will affect him more than other people all his life; what would be nothing to an ordinary person might kill him.'

Mrs. Quitchett sat down on a seat near, rather hastily, and looked hard out, up the path.

'You don't mean to say he's in any danger?' she said.

'Danger, dear, dear, no! Don't run away with any notion of that sort. The child has a skin scratch that is half healed already; that's all. I only mean that, considering how very slightly he's hurt, it's odd he isn't running about again as well as ever. The boy must have an odd constitution.'

'He was never remarkably strong,' Mrs. Quitchett answered, with a touch of irony; 'the wonder was that we reared him. Such a baby as he was! you didn't know if you had him in your arms or not. But she was a good nurser, though I verily believe she'd have had a wet-nurse if I hadn't shamed her out of it. She said the babe was a drag on her; she didn't let him stay so long, poor lamb. He owes what health he's got to you and me, sir, under Providence, though I say it that should not.' Mrs. Quitchett was not a great talker as a rule, certainly no gossip, and probably to no one but so old a friend as the doctor would she have touched on the subject of Mrs. Ebbesley's shortcomings.

'Well, nurse,' said the doctor cheerfully, 'still under Providence, we'll have him healthier yet before we've done with him; depend on it, he'll bury many stronger people.'

But Mrs. Quitchett laid by the doctor's words in her heart. 'What would be nothing to an ordinary person might kill him.' The sentence made a place for itself deep in her memory, to be recalled only too well years after it was spoken. She had a great regard for the doctor,—he was one of the few people whose opinion she respected, —and she whispered to herself as she got Tim's tea ready, 'He tried to smooth it away, but it's better to face things. He means what he says, for he's a man of sense, which is more than most.' Some relic of her anxiety must have lingered in her face when she carried in the little tray, for Tim said, 'Why, nurse, how grave you look; what's doctor been telling you?' but broke off to add, 'Please, I want you to let *him* stay to tea with me; may he?' 'Him' was Carol, who was there again, to inquire after Tim's progress, and whom that youth was still very shy of mentioning by name. Carol came nearly every day now, and his visits did more for Tim than either the doctor's medicine or Mrs. Darley's jelly.

'Master Darley can have his tea with you and welcome, if he thinks his grandmamma would not object,' said Mrs. Quitchett, glad, as on a former occasion, to escape the first of Tim's questions by answering the second,— glad too of any chance to make the boy look so happy.

Carol had a fine appetite and ate more than his host, in spite of the dinner that would follow, for him, by and by.

'Do you never eat more than that?' he asked in wondering pity.

'Oh yes, sometimes I eat a great deal, when I've been running about,' answered Tim.

'He makes a hearty tea mostly,' added Mrs. Quitchett, 'though he never was much of a boy for his dinner.' Tim sighed; he began to fear he was not 'much of a boy' for anything. He had never thought about himself before, but Carol seemed to present a standard by which to measure creation, and he felt for his part that he fell far short of the desired point. Carol's next question was not calculated to reassure him; it was one boys always ask, and grown-up men too sometimes, and is of all others the most difficult to answer—

'What do you do with yourself all day?'

Now Tim's days were always well filled, but on a sudden it seemed to him that none of his pursuits were worthy of mention, so he said the best thing he could under the circumstances—

'I don't know; I never thought; sometimes I do one thing, sometimes another.'

'Do you read much? Ain't you dull all by yourself?'

'Oh no, I'm never dull. I like reading; not geography and that sort of thing; I hate that, but fairy-tales. Do you read the *Arabian Nights*?'

'Yes, I've read some. I like Aladdin: what a clever chap he was. What else do you do?'

'Oh! I get flowers, and I find out new walks, and make-believe seeking adventures, and I tell stories to Bess,' says Tim, grown bolder.

'What, the dog? What a rum idea!'

Tim felt he had said something foolish. 'Do you care for flowers?' he said hastily.

'Yes, I'm very fond of them; Aunt Kate is teaching me botany.'

'I don't know what that is,' says downright Tim, 'but I'm glad you like flowers. I was afraid you wouldn't care for them; that you'd think it was childish or something.'

'Not I. I bet I could beat you at the names of wildflowers; but I like birds better. Our keeper knows birds by their flight, and I do some of 'em now. I've got a cabinet of eggs. I'll show you when you come and see me.' Tim was grateful and interested.

'Oh! and I tell you what—you shall help me with my telegraph; I've got a telegraph from one tree to another, made with string and a basket; but it's no fun sending messages to oneself, and Aunt Kate's no good at climbing trees.'

'I'm afraid I shouldn't be much.'

'Oh yes you will; I'll show you how, and you shall have the easy tree. I'm afraid it's too far, or we'd have a telegraph from our house to this, but I should never get enough string.' And so the talk would go on, with, 'Oh! do you do that? so do I,' and 'Oh! that's just what I always think,' — delightful discoveries of unexpected sympathies, in spite of great unlikeness in most things, and innocent remarks on Tim's part, which made Carol shout with laughter, and then stop and explain very kindly and carefully why he was amused, as he saw the pained look spring into his friend's face at his mirth.

'Do you play games?' he asked once.

'I don't care much for games,' Tim answered innocently, 'but I play draughts sometimes of an evening with Mrs. Quitchett.'

'Oh! I didn't mean *that* sort of game,' said Carol; 'I meant cricket and that sort of thing; the kind of games we play at school.'

'No,' Tim owned reluctantly; 'you see I've had no one to play with, but I should like to learn, if you'll teach me.'

'Oh yes, I'll teach you; of course you couldn't have learnt with no one to play with. Mrs. Quitchett doesn't look as if she'd be much good at bowling,' and then both boys laughed.

'By the way,' Carol asked, after a little, 'how comes it that you and she live here all alone? She's no relation of yours, is she?'

'No, she's my nurse,—was, you know, of course I mean.' Tim was beginning to be dimly conscious that as Carol had no nurse, it was not the right thing. 'But,' he added with compunction at disowning dear Mrs. Quitchett, 'I love her as if she was my mother.'

'And is your mother dead?'

'I don't know; I think I never had a mother.'

'Oh, you must have had one. I suppose she's dead; mine is—my father too'; and a sweet gravity stole over the bright young face.

'Poor dear.' said Tim, forgetting in his pity for his friend that he was himself far more alone in the world. He accepted Carol's explanation of the utter absence of his mother from his life, supposing him right on all subjects. 'She must have died when you were a baby, before you could remember; they do sometimes,' his instructor had said; he knew so much more than Tim about everything. That youth believed in him firmly. 'Carol says so,' became a formula with which he would confront Mrs. Quitchett herself, who smiled superior, but left him his comfortable reliance.

The wisdom of Solomon was nothing in Tim's eyes to that of this radiant being, who was not only a proficient in such unknown arts as cricket, but actually beat him on his own ground of wildflowers and fairy-tales, having acquired a smattering of Greek mythology endlessly astonishing and delightful. Had any one dared to deny that Carol was the born prince of all mankind, I don't know what Tim would have said to him. He counted the hours between his friend's visits, brightened visibly when he came into the room, seemed to lose all heart when he left it, and watched his every motion with looks of jealous love. Carol, on his side, grew to have quite a protecting kindness for the pale child, perhaps not sorry to show off a little to such an appreciative audience; finding Tim too not an unpleasant novelty and variation from the companionlessness of the Court.

It was getting on towards October now, but Tim had entirely forgotten the approaching advent of his father, so completely did Carol engross all his thoughts, until one day Carol himself was the means of recalling it to him.

'Where's your father?' he asked, pausing in an attempt to reproduce the features of Bess on a small lump of wax used by Mrs. Quitchett for waxing her thread, with the aid of that lady's best scissors.

'He's in India,' answered Tim, mechanically giving the reply always given to him; and then remembering suddenly his father's letter, 'At least.' he added, 'I believe he's coming home soon. I must ask Mrs. Quitchett when he's coming.'

'What! don't you know? Why didn't you tell me? Shan't you be glad to see him?' persists inquisitive Carol.

'I don't think I care much: don't believe I ever did see him.'

'And how do you know he's coming?'

'I forget: dreamed it, I fancy; or else Mrs. Quitchett had it in a letter.'

'That's more likely, I should think,' said Carol, laughing; and so the matter dropped, Mrs. Quitchett not being at hand for reference as to date. And that was the only occasion on which Mr. Ebbesley's name was mentioned between the two boys. The circles widened round it in Tim's memory like those round a pebble in a stream till they merged by degrees into the even flow of his new friendship.

Mrs. Quitchett, on the contrary, who had not made a new friend these twenty years, had wondered several times that she received no second letter from her employer; wondered too, not without misgiving, what he would think of the Court intimacy, but felt it was none of her doing, so put it aside among the things to be accepted, not curable, even if harmful, by any amount of speculation.

One day—the 16ᵗʰ of September I think it was—a heavy gray day, dull and cheerless, when out of doors felt like a stuffy room, and Mrs. Quitchett said there was thunder in the air, Tim was restless and uncomfortable. In vain his nurse had tried to interest him in his accustomed pursuits. Pari-banou could do nothing for him; he had grown tired of drawing princes and princesses with strange sausage-shaped bodies and long elbowless arms that projected before and behind; and still Carol did not come. The days were getting shorter now, and there was not much of the afternoon left.

Ah! there he comes at last. The gate swings creaking, and Carol, hot and breathless, stirs the air in the dull house with his lusty cry of 'Tim, where are you?' 'Yes, he knows he is late; he's very sorry, but he had much to do; has been, among other things, to get some blackberries, and has brought them to Tim.'—not quite all, perhaps, to judge from certain stains on the fair face, unless he picked them with his teeth, but still a goodly show of squashy purple berries in a pocket-handkerchief;—Tim must have them for his tea; yes, that will be delightful, and Carol will stop and help eat them.

'I've been out in the garden to-day,' Tim says; 'the Virginia creeper is quite red in some places, and there is hardly a rose left.'

'The time's getting on, and that reminds me I had something to ask you: will you take care of my squirrel for me when I go away? He doesn't want much looking after, — only nuts, and to have the hay changed for his bed once in three days. Hulloa! don't you feel well? shall I call Mrs. Quitchett?'

'No, no, I'm all right; but what did you say? are you going away?'

'Oh, is that all? I thought you knew it; I must have told you; every one else knows it: I'm going to Eton next week; didn't I tell you?'

'No — you — didn't — tell — me.' poor Tim answered very slowly. 'You talked about school, but — but — I don't know — I didn't think; I thought you'd always come and see me.'

'Oh! never mind, you know,' Carol said, rather disturbed at this unexpected effect of his announcement; 'you'll get on all right; and then I shall write, and the holidays'll come in no time, and all that.'

The consolation was vague, but effectual. After all, the separation would not be eternal, and there would be the squirrel. Would Tim take care of him? wouldn't he? How that squirrel got over-fed when he came to live at the manor-house!

Once started on the subject of going to Eton, Carol had much to tell, and Tim was a wonderful listener. This was Carol's first promotion from the ranks of a private school, second only in importance to that of having a gun. The topic lasted through tea, and was still engrossing them when they were startled by the sound of wheels, which stopped at the gate.

'What can it be?' said Tim; 'the doctor's not coming to-day.' Tim was lying on the sofa, and Carol sitting beside him. They heard some unwonted commotion in the hall, and Mrs. Quitchett's voice in accents of keenest surprise.

Carol jumped up and was for going to see what had happened; but he had not long to wait, for the next moment the door opened, and he found himself struggling fiercely in the arms of a tall yellow-faced gentleman, with grizzled hair and whiskers, who was straining him passionately to his heart.

'Let me go; what are you doing?' he called out, kicking frantically; and Tim, supposing some damage was intended to his idol, set up a feeble wail. It was at this moment that Mrs. Quitchett entered, and called out —

'Law, Mr. Ebbesley, sir, that's young Master Darley from the Court you've got hold of.' Then pointing to the sofa, where Tim lay crying, whiter and thinner even than usual, she added, 'That one's your son.'

CHAPTER IV

This child is not mine as the first was,
I cannot sing it to rest:
I cannot lift it up fatherly
And bless it upon my breast.

Lowell's *Changeling*.

William Ebbesley had travelled night and day. As he neared the child that was all he had left on earth, for whose sake he had lived loveless for seven years of incessant work, his impatience for his reward increased. He outstripped the post, writing letters but not lingering for them to be received. What did it matter whether they were prepared for him on this day or that? had not they been waiting for him for months past? He had meant to wander through France and Italy on his way; to visit Rome, Venice, Paris; to turn aside here and there, as fancy led him. The thought of ease and leisure was pleasant to the weary wayfarer on life's highway; he, whose whole time had for years been portioned out with the regularity and monotony of clockwork, found, or expected to find, a luxury in caprice and idleness. But the thought of his boy drove all others from his head. They would see Europe together, and all wonders of nature or of art should steal a fresh charm for him, mirrored in the delight of young eyes. His wanderings would be far more pleasantly irregular, dictated by the wayward fancy of a bright impulsive child, than by his own more conventional judgment.

Mr. Ebbesley's expectations of his son were not bounded by strict reason: he did not reflect that the child had never even heard of most of the countries they were to visit. His life had not favoured much exercise of the imagination, and all he possessed of that quality had flowed for seven years in this one direction. It was art, literature, and all to him; and we have seen how widely the conception he had built up for himself differed from the reality. The child of his dreams must be tall, well-made and bright-coloured, merry and healthy, but above all he must be full to overflowing with love to match the love he was bringing him. He knew nothing of children, and drew his conclusions about a child of nine from the feelings of his own heart at fifty, never doubting that on the boy's side the meeting had been as eagerly looked for as on his. He had never learnt that to a child a mere name such as 'Father' cannot endear a person he has never seen. Those he is with, from whom he receives kindness, however slight, may count upon his warmest affection; but tell him he must love one brought to him for the first time because he is akin to him, and he will not understand the claim.

The drive from Granthurst Station in the crawling fly had seemed endless to the poor man. Have we not all had those drives, when we felt how much faster we could go on foot, yet knew we could not? He had walked up all the hills, in hopes that the wretched asthmatic old horse would gain more energy for going down on the other side. And at last he was here — here on the threshold of happiness, hardly daring to turn the handle of the door. When he entered the room he never doubted for an instant which of the boys before him was his son; indeed Carol, standing in the centre of the room, was an object which so effectually caught the eye, that Tim, lying prone upon the sofa, in the shadow of its high back, was scarcely noticeable. He did not stop to consider that Carol was some four years older than his son could possibly be; it was quite in accordance with his views that the boy should be tall for his age, and in all other respects the lad before him realised so completely the picture of his child which for years had made itself in his heart.

Who can blame him for the sinking he experienced as, following the outstretched arm of the nurse, his eyes rested on the little figure of Tim? He put down the offended Carol without a word of apology, and stood looking at his son: he was too much taken aback to make any demonstration. His pent-up feelings had expended themselves in the passionate clasp of Carol to his breast. Had he found Tim alone, those feelings must yet have found vent, and would, if they had not counteracted his disappointment, at least have softened it: his fancy would have been busy to make excuses to itself for the child which was, though it was not, the original of his dream-child. But now fate had shown him the perfect realisation of his hopes and wishes, only to pluck it away and substitute this changeling in its place.

As for poor Tim, he was dimly conscious that something was wrong. This tall, gray-headed stranger, who was yet his father, frightened him; he felt the disappointment in those sad cold eyes, though he could not understand it. For hardly more than a minute the father and son looked at one another, but the chill of that minute was as a barrier between them through all their after-intercourse.

At length, roused by some gesture or sound of Mrs. Quitchett's to a sense of what was required of him, William Ebbesley stooped and kissed Tim's forehead, and then left the room without a word. It was necessary for him to be alone, to arrange the crowding thoughts that pressed upon his brain, to think, to determine—above all, to be master of himself. Half an hour afterwards, when Mrs. Quitchett went to seek him in the room to which he had gone—a little chamber by the front door, which had been his study in the old days—she found him sitting still in his coat as he had come in.

'I came to see if you wouldn't take something to eat, sir; I'm sorry we were so unready for you, but if you wrote I never got it, though I wondered not to hear from you again.'

He raised his head, and answered her almost mechanically, 'Oh yes, he would have something, no matter what—whatever was least trouble.' She brought him the little meal she had arranged for him, and stood watching him as he ate in silence, with the air of one doing accustomed things in his sleep. Her loving old heart had lent keenness to her sight, and she had seen at a glance how things stood; she longed to smooth matters a little, but hardly knew how to begin; she had always had some awe of her master, which time and distance had not diminished, and at present he seemed in no mood for conversation. Presently she took courage and spoke. 'You mustn't think, sir, the little one won't be very glad to see you, when he finds himself a bit; the poor dear's not himself; he had an accident a fortnight or so back, and he's weak and nervous yet. Your coming was sudden to him, poor dear—'

He interrupted her almost angrily. 'Who did you say that other boy was?'

"Tis young Master Darley, sir, from the Court; it was he that caused your son's accident while shooting, and he's been nearly every day since to sit with him.'

'He mustn't come any more.'

Mrs. Quitchett was horrified. 'Your son'll fret to death without him,' she said; 'he's going away to school soon; let him come till then.'

She knew what had passed in her master's mind, and did not attempt to argue with him; only she begged for a little reprieve for her darling, who was more precious in her eyes than all the healthiest children in England. Mr. Ebbesley considered a little and then answered, 'Very well; but don't let *me* see him.' And with that Mrs. Quitchett was fain to be content.

Tim meanwhile clung to Carol. 'Don't leave me,' he said, again and again; 'he frightens me, that man. I don't care if he is my father; I want you, and only you. I don't care about him'; and then again, 'Promise me you won't leave me, Carol; always be my friend.'

Carol promised readily enough—would have promised anything just then to get away. He did not like emotional display, and he was very angry with Mr. Ebbesley. 'Was that old man mad?' he said indignantly as he scudded off homewards. But his wrath was not of a kind upon which the sun goes down, and the air and exercise soon restored him to his usual spirits. A little breeze had come up towards sunset, and blew refreshingly in his flushed face. 'How hot that room was!'

And here for a time we must part company with him. With the evening wind in his curls, he springs out of our story, and is lost to our eyes for a little. Two days later he went to Eton. Tim heard the Court dogcart whirl by the house, on its way to the station. Did Carol look round? Was that his hand waving? He could not quite tell, for his eyes were full of childish tears.

Soon after this Tim was about again as usual. A man had brought the squirrel in his cage, with a message of farewell, from its owner. But for that, life seemed much the same as before. Had he dreamed all this, as he lay on the high-backed sofa?

At first even the presence of his father in the house made but little difference: when they met, Tim never showed to advantage; he was frightened, and his scared manner irritated Mr. Ebbesley, who never guessed how much character he had. The poor man had no notion how to talk to the child. He patted him stiffly on the head, and asked him questions that he could not answer. He was like a man who, meeting another in some foreign country, wishes to hold converse with him, but does not know in what language to address him. If the boy would but begin, he thought, — would seem in any way glad to have him there, or claim his interest in his pursuits, he could respond, and would. He almost wished him to be naughty; he knew he could reprove him, and that at least would be intercourse, and might lead to something else; only this simple shyness and silence he was powerless to attack. On one point he had no doubt. The life his son was leading was a most unprofitable one, and a radical change must be made in it; he called him into his study and told him so. Tim naturally had not the least idea of what he meant. He looked very uncomfortable, and pulled Bess's ears.

'Your education,' his father went on, 'has been sadly neglected; if you are ever to know what other people do, it is time you should begin to learn something.'

Tim, seeing something was expected of him, whispered, 'Yes, sir.'

'Don't call me "sir,"' said Mr. Ebbesley shortly; 'it sounds common. I had thought of sending you to school, but as you are very backward, and your nurse tells me you are not strong, I have decided to keep you at home and give you a tutor for the present. I have engaged a gentleman who will come here next week.'

Tim gasped: here was a revolution. 'You don't mean Mr. Brown?' he asked. Mr. Brown was the village schoolmaster.

'I know of no such person; that is not your tutor's name.'

'Oh!'

'You can read, I suppose?'

'Yes.'

'What has Mr. Brown taught you? I suppose he is the schoolmaster.'

'A little jography, and sums.'

Mr. Ebbesley hesitated for a moment as to whether it was not his duty to examine his son in these branches of knowledge, but came to the conclusion it was not. 'His tutor will do all that when he comes,' he thought 'You may go now,' he said aloud. Tim needed no urging, but was out of the room at once. On the door-mat, however, he paused; something perplexed him: he went through a fearful struggle with himself, then he knocked; he was actuated by a strong desire to do right, and give satisfaction. He heard his father say 'Come in,' and saw the surprised look on his face when he saw who had knocked. Tim stood in the doorway.

'Well?' said Mr. Ebbesley.

'If you please,' said Tim, 'you said I wasn't to call you "sir"; what shall I call you?'

'Is the boy half-witted? Call me? Why, "father," of course; what else would you call me?' And as the door closed again, he said to himself sadly, 'Fancy a child that does not *know* what to call his own father! Is this what I have worked and waited for?'

How came it that these two, having each such a wealth of affection to bestow, could not spend it on one another? On the father's side it seemed to congeal in his heart; on the son's it found vent in a passionate devotion to almost the only being capable of inspiring it, who had crossed his lonely little path. To the birds, to Bess, to the brook in the woods he unburthened his heart, and babbled of Carol. But to no living person did he mention his name, insomuch that even Mrs. Quitchett thought he had forgotten him. One great treasure he possessed. Not long after his friend had gone to Eton, the Court groom brought a letter that had come for Tim from Carol, enclosed in one to Mrs. Darley. It was written in a big schoolboy hand, and told how the writer was well, and hoped Tim was, and how he liked Eton, and found lots of fellows who had been at his last school; and some day he hoped Tim would come there, when he was a big fellow. Tim should be his fag. He fagged for Ward, who was captain of the house. He liked football, — that is the lower-boy games, for in the house games the big fellows had it all their own way, and it was a bore never touching the ball; and he remained Tim's affectionate friend, Carol Darley. And, P.S. he hoped Tim would be careful not to turn the cage round when the squirrel was half through the hole into the sleeping-place.

Tim was ashamed to answer this, for though love of story-books had early induced him to master reading, his writing was in a painfully rudimentary state; and as little boys at Eton do not write, as a rule, for pure love of the thing, the letter had no successors. But it supplied Tim with a motive for working with the new tutor in a way that astonished that gentleman, who did not know that his object was to fit himself for Eton before such time as Carol should be old enough to leave.

Tim's tutor does not require any minute description at our hands; he was one of those extraordinary men who, though elegant scholars and, in a way, profound thinkers, have yet missed the rewards obtained by men much less gifted than themselves, and are glad of such hack-work as the temporary education of the Tims of this world. It was a relief to him to find that his pupil was only backward, not incurably dull, as were most of the lads into whom it had been his painful duty to hammer the rudiments of many useless branches of knowledge.

Still, although he took a genuine interest in his charge, which Tim repaid by a grateful feeling very near affection and wonderfully good behaviour, he neither had nor desired any insight into the child's heart. Some men are born without a fondness for children, just as some have no ear for music; their more favoured brethren look down on them with sublime contempt, but it is absurd to blame either one or the other. Altogether, except as the means of enabling him to prepare for what he so ardently desired, this blameless, learned fellow-creature played but a small part in the life of our hero. That life, but for this new element of education, was for the present much unchanged. After the installation of the tutor, Tim saw but little of his father, which he scarcely regretted. Mr. Ebbesley was often away for weeks at a time, being interested in his profession and watching many cases carefully. Gradually he began to get briefs himself, and established chambers in London, where he spent most of his time; his tastes were not countrified. Mr. Darley had called and had asked him to dine at the Court, but the talk there was so exclusively of Carol, of his letters, his beauty, his skill in games, and thousand virtues, that it almost maddened the poor man.

'You saw our boy before he went away,' the Squire said; 'he has taken quite a fancy for your little fellow. We owe Mr. Ebbesley apologies, my dear, for that unfortunate accident; and yet,' he added graciously, 'we mustn't call it unfortunate if it makes us all better acquainted.'

'Thank you,' answered his victim, to whom the Squire's milk of human kindness was very sour indeed; 'daresay your grandson was glad to find a young companion,' He detected a spice of pity in the reference to Tim which was far from pleasing him.

'Oh well, you know,' said grandpapa, 'I think he felt very sorry for having been the innocent cause of such a mishap; he has a good heart, that boy, and is as tender as a girl for anything in pain, though he's a brave boy too. But nothing would satisfy him but that we must send to inquire the same afternoon. He has a spice of Darley obstinacy in him.'

'I don't think you can call it obstinacy, dear,' put in grandmamma; 'I'm sure he's not a difficult child to guide if you're judicious with him. When he was quite a little tiny thing I always said, "That's a child that can be ruled by kindness and no other way, for he has a high spirit." I recollect when he first went to the school he was at, before Eton, I went down there, and the schoolmaster said to me—I forget his name. Kate dear, do you remember his name? was it Watt or Watkin? Watson, was it? Are you sure? Well, it doesn't matter—Mr. Watson said, "He's not a bad boy, Mrs. Darley, but very self-willed."—"No, Mr. Watkins," I said, "*there* you must allow me to correct you; *not* self-willed, only with a great deal of spirit," and I'm sure I was right. And your poor dear little boy? I hope he's quite well again; he didn't look at all strong.'

'Yes, he's quite strong and hearty again, thank you; it was a mere nothing.'

'Oh, I'm glad to hear it; to me he looked delicate, but then they say I'm always saying people are ill. May he come and see us sometimes? but perhaps he'd not care to, now Carol is away; the house is dull without him.'

'You are very good, but he is hard at work just now, and I am afraid I must ask you to excuse him. I have got him a tutor, and he is pursuing a more regular course of life than has been possible hitherto. Will that branch line the railway talk of making touch your property in any way, Mr. Darley?' plunging wildly away from the subject. It seemed as if they were galling him on purpose; and when the Squire made one of his old-fashioned courtly speeches to the effect that 'if the more exciting sports of India had not rendered their homely partridge and pheasant shooting too tame for him, he hoped he would bring his gun.' etc., he answered bluntly that he had given up shooting, and so said good-night.

'A very curt person,' said Mrs. Darley; 'I am sure, if only in common gratitude to that dear boy for all his goodness to little what's-his-name, he ought to be more civil. Fancy a little thing like that working hard! I only hope his father doesn't beat him.'

And so gradually the intercourse between the two houses languished considerably.

The morning after the dinner at the Court Mr. Ebbesley encountered Tim, his lessons done, flying out of the house in his usual hat-less condition. The conversation of the Darleys was still rankling, and his tone was not gentle as he said—

'You've forgotten your hat.'

'I never wear one except on Sunday,' answered Tim simply.

'Not wear a hat!' ejaculated his father. 'I never heard of such a thing; I desire you will begin at once.'

'But they are so uncomfortable,' said poor Tim.

'I think really it's time you left off such childish nonsense,' answered Mr. Ebbesley, now really provoked. 'Why can't you do as other people do? Why should my son go tearing about like a butcher-boy more than other people's? It was evidently high time I came home.'

Tim gave in and promised compliance. Carol, he remembered, wore a hat, and of course he would have to when he went to Eton, but it was pain and grief to him. Clearly the days of liberty were over; hats and the Latin grammar were beginning to plough on Tim's back and make long furrows. Meanwhile he had discovered, Heaven knows how, the date when the Eton holidays should begin, and he kept strict record of the days on a scrap of paper, scoring off one each night when he went to bed.

At last came the long-looked-for 14th of December, and with it Carol; and now for a time Tim was really happy. All the time he could spare from his lessons was spent in trotting about after his friend like a little dog. Wherever Carol led Tim followed, though his soul quaked within him at some of his own exploits. Only when Carol rode upon his pony Tim could not accompany him; and later in the holidays, when a school-fellow of his own age came on a visit to the elder boy, he grew, boylike, a little ashamed of the constant companionship of such a child as Tim, which the latter needed no hints to tell him. But in spite of drawbacks—and what in this world is perfect?—these were among the happiest weeks in our hero's life. At no later time did he have again such unrestrained opportunities of worshipping his idol.

Mrs. Quitchett watched all this with an apprehensive eye. No touch of jealousy mingled in her pure devoted love for the child of her heart, but she trembled lest some blow should lie in store for him, that should strike him through this new affection; she did not forget, as Tim seemed to have done, that first evening of Mr, Ebbesley's arrival. At each of that gentleman's visits from London she feared some renewal of the talk they had had on that occasion,—some fresh decree of banishment against the unconscious intruder. That his company should be unwelcome to any one was an idea that circumstances had combined to prevent from ever entering Carol's head, but he did not like Mr. Ebbesley, and so timed his visits mostly when he was not at the manor-house, to Mrs. Quitchett's great relief; and whatever Mr. Ebbesley may have thought, he said nothing, and the holidays passed over without mishap. Golden days to Tim, speeding by as such days are only too apt to speed, never to come back any more. Indeed, it was some time before the boys met again.

When Easter brought Carol back to Darley, he found the manor-house shut up; only Bess, wandering disconsolately, came and wagged her tail at sight of an acquaintance. Mr. Ebbesley had taken his son for that continental tour to which he had so long looked forward. It would be hard to say what odd quirk in the man made him cling to this part of his old dream, now that so much of it had gone astray; perhaps he had a sort of hope that change of air and scene might develop Tim into something more like what he had imagined him, — that by adhering rigidly to his programme some result that he had looked for might follow even yet.

And, indeed, in the strange new world to which he was transported, Tim found much to excite and interest him. Mr. Ebbesley was better pleased with him than he had been yet, but by this time it was too late for him to overcome the feeling of constraint and fear he always felt in his father's presence. He was never at his ease with him. And then he was such a child, so very young. He could not appreciate half he saw. But William Ebbesley did not understand all that, and there was no one to tell it to him.

At midsummer it was Carol who was absent. A visit to a friend's house, measles in the village — I know Tim had them slightly about that time, — a journey to Scotland with his grandparents, and the six weeks' holiday was gone without bringing him to the Court. It was a year before Tim saw Carol again. A year, which is so little to older people, is a very long time at Tim's age — a long time for a little boy to remain fixed in his loyalty to an idea. But Tim remained fixed for that year and for others that followed, there being no one to disturb his allegiance. Carol was his almanac, all minor events dating from the periods when he was with him.

How eagerly he longed for the day which, by taking him to Eton, should put an end to the long separations; he feared nothing that might await him there, for he would be near Carol always then, and what more could he want than that?

CHAPTER V

Oh! better than the world of dress,
And pompous dining-out;
Better than simpering and finesse,
Is all this stir and rout.
    — *Ionica.*

It was a proud day for Tim when his tutor announced that he considered him sufficiently well grounded to take Fourth Form at Eton. Tim was now twelve years old, and had adopted a more virile costume than the holland blouse of his youth. But for that and his little learning, he was quite unchanged from what we have known him. It is circumstances and events that make people young or old, not the years that pass over their heads. Some few happy people never grow up, but are boys and girls at heart all their lives. Few of us can have reached maturity without remembering periods when we have felt very old, and the pleasant shock of getting younger again; and even in the oldest people's lives, little patches of youth blossom out now and then. But in boys the differences are even more marked. Some are little men from the time they can walk, with all a man's self-reliance and self-conceit; others ripen very slowly; some hardly at all.

Carol, who had been to school, and lived among older people, had fancied himself quite grown up at twelve. He dined downstairs and went out shooting, and talked of Tim, as I have said, as 'poor child.' But Tim at the same age was as much a child as he had been at nine or eight or seven. Any one less fitted to be put down suddenly in all the stir and hubbub and seeming heartlessness of a big public school, it would be hard to find. But then Tim knew nothing of public school life; to him going to Eton meant only reunion with Carol. Mr. Ebbesley was astonished at the boy's eagerness; he knew him to be shy and rather nervous, and could not conceive what made him desire a way of life so unlike anything which might naturally have been supposed to be congenial to him. He set it down with characteristic morbidness partly to a desire to get away from him; but on the whole he was pleased at the wish, as manifesting a spirit more like other boys than he was wont to find in his small son. Mr. Darley had recommended his grandson's tutor to his neighbour; so, to Tim's great joy, he found himself one bright May morning actually an Eton boy, and an inmate of the same house as Carol.

That youth was sixteen now, and in Middle Division; and any one more versed than Tim in the manners and customs of the strange world into which he had been transported, could have told him that whatever hopes he might cherish of companionship were doomed to disappointment. Between a white-tied young man in Carol's position, and a little scug in Fourth Form there is a great gulf fixed.

That first day at school seemed interminable in its dreary emptiness to the new boy. He had a shadowy feeling that something fearful would happen if he were a minute late for the time at which he was told to present himself in school, and dared settle to no employment, for fear that hour should come, and pass unheeded; and in the meanwhile the long unemployed interval stretched away dismally before him. A hundred times he pulled out the new silver watch his father had bought for him, to find that just five minutes had elapsed since he last consulted it. He ventured a little way up town, and then came back and started afresh, but the sense of his costume, so new to him, so familiar to the passers-by, made him feel as if every eye must be upon him, and he again sought refuge in his bare little chamber. He felt so terribly alone and uncared-for. He heard voices and hurrying steps in the echoing wooden passages, and then a silence succeeded, which filled him with terror lest some school was going on which he ought to be attending. He crept along the passage and peeped into one or two open doors; there were boots lying about, and little heaps of clothes: the boys had gone to their games and a noontide stillness reigned through the big house. Down in the yard under his window the shoeblack was singing a cheerful vulgar song as he cleaned the knives, sometimes interrupted by calling to a brother menial, invisible in the inner regions of pantry, scraps of light badinage or local gossip. Tim would have liked to descend and chat with them, — anything to break the sense of being dead and forgotten that weighed upon his soul.

Only the little boys were back as yet. Carol was coming that evening, Tim told himself, and then he would lose this strange feeling of isolation; he had a vague notion that Carol would devote at least the first day to taking him about and showing him the place. 'It's a pity we couldn't have come back together,' he thought; but Carol had explained to him that it was unheard-of for any boy to return before his proper time. The weary day wore itself out at last, but still Carol had not arrived. Supper-time, prayer-time, bed-time, so the boys' maid announced to Tim who was sitting up, though it was hard work to keep the heavy eyelids from closing. 'What, not in bed yet, sir? why, it's past ten. I must take your light in another five minutes. Now make 'aste and get to bed; you're as sleepy as ever you can be; we can't 'ave you little ones sitting up like this; there's trouble enough to get the lights from the big gentlemen without that.' Subsequent angry altercations in the passage proved to Tim the truth of the good lady's assertion. He obeyed, not having courage to question the mandate of this peremptory person, but it was sorely against his will. Carol would think it so unkind of him, he was afraid, not to have sat up for him. But perhaps he would come to see *him*, just to say he had come, and good-night. So he forced himself to keep awake; he knew there was a train in about half-past ten, and it was almost that before his light was taken. Between sleeping and waking he was conscious of the sound of wheels, of voices and laughter under his window, then luggage was dragged with many thumps along the passage. Tim was wide awake again now, listening with all ears. Three or four boys just come were going to their rooms, full of talk, loth to separate, having many things to say. Suddenly, — yes, that was Carol's voice, talking eagerly, questioning, answering, laughing. Tim sat up ready to call out that he was awake, though the room was dark, the moment the door opened; he never doubted it *would* open. The talkers seemed to pause just outside his room. 'I swear you've got fat; hasn't he?' 'What have you been doing with yourself?' Then a shout. 'Why, if it isn't the hyena! Come to my arms, hyena; how's your old self? Oh! I say, come to my room; I've got something to show you, if I can find it. Never mind, Martha; it's the first night, you know, and we shan't be long.' Then the voices, still talking, turned the corner and grew fainter as the boys retreated. Tim sat up in the dark, still waiting, still hoping. The house wasn't quiet yet; little bursts of merriment reached him yet occasionally, and Martha's voice raised in bitter expostulation. Then more steps, renewed hope, fresh disappointment, and silence and blackness once more. I am much afraid that amid the renewing of so many interrupted interests, and meeting of so many former friends, Carol had forgotten the existence of his little new schoolfellow. He remembered him next morning though, and went in search of him.

'Hulloa, well, here you are,' he said not unkindly, but with some embarrassment, after he had shaken hands, and while he wandered round the little room examining everything minutely, as a cover for his want of conversation. 'I suppose you'll soon shake in, you know, and make friends. Come to me if you want to know anything, and if anyone bullies you — badly — just you let me know; but no one will: this isn't the sort of house. Nothing I can do for you?' The truth was he was debating uneasily what he *could* do for Tim. He had often been asked to 'look after' boys before, with whose parents he had some acquaintance, and in such cases he had always asked the boy to breakfast, and having been bored for half an hour, considered his duty done, and thought no more about him. But

Tim was different; and then you couldn't ask a lower boy in your own house to breakfast, especially if he was going to be your fag by and by.

So that Tim rather weighed on Carol's soul with a sense of ill-defined responsibility. He wondered whether he oughtn't to explain things to him, but didn't know how to begin; he felt it would be absurd to preach him a sort of little sermon.

'I suppose you know pretty well about things,' he said vaguely, with a rather doubtful glance.

'Yes, I think so, thank you, Carol.'

'Oh! and I say, you know,' the elder lad rejoined carelessly, 'you won't think it unkind, you know; but you'll have to call me Darley here, you know; of course it won't make any difference in the holidays; but it wouldn't do, don't you see.'

Tim promised to remember, and Carol departed feeling relieved, after a parting injunction not to 'sock away all his money.'

'What is one to do,' he asked of his chief friend and crony Villidge minor, as they strolled together arm in arm towards chapel, 'with a small boy in one's own house that one knows at home?'

'If it's a riddle I give it up; if not, I should say kick him,' answered Villidge cheerfully.

'No, but seriously, you know,' persisted Carol, anxious to do his duty.

'Why, seriously, what *can* you do? Nothing. Wholesome neglect, my friend, is the one valid principle of education.'

So Carol laughed and determined to act on the one valid principle, the advice being thoroughly in accordance with his own views of the subject.

'That's what old Blow-hard (by which name he designated one of his preceptors) would call the great "Layssy fair" of Political Economists,' he said. 'What a mercy we're not up to him this half!' and so the talk drifted into other channels.

Tim saw him at dinner sitting far off at another table, but when Carol looked round to the corner where the new boys sat, and nodded encouragingly, the attention thus attracted to him made him so shy, that he almost wished he had remained undistinguished. When the meal was over, and he was retreating once more, he found himself the centre of an unoccupied and inquisitive group of lower boys, who were giving themselves airs in the passage, in the temporary absence of their social superiors.

'Hulloa, new fellow, what's your name?'

'Where have you taken?'

'Where do you board?' added a wag, affecting ignorance of the house he was in.

At this they all laughed, and some one added —

'Do you know Darley at home?'

'Yes.'

'Happy Darley.'

'Shut up, Carter; you're a deal too clever; some day you'll do yourself an injury if you don't look out.'

'Come and look at the papers, Weston,' returned Carter hastily, who was nervous when Weston began to chaff him, and proud of taking an interest in public affairs in advance of most of his contemporaries. 'The big fellows choke up the library all day, and look thunder if a lower boy comes in.'

'They are very welcome,' said Weston, who liked shocking Carter. 'I'm not going to waste a precious after-two so early in the half when I've still got some tin; it don't hold out long. Besides, the *Times* has gone off; it used to be full of assizes, and now it's all politics and that sort of rot.'

'The *Police News* is Tommy's favourite paper, isn't it, Tommy? Never mind, sock us an ice and I'll come with you, and Carter shall do politics for the lot of us.'

At this point the projects, literary and otherwise, of the party were rudely broken in upon by the unwelcome sound of 'Lower boy-hoy-hoy,' roared lustily from the landing above in a fine fresh young bass before which the trebles ceased to pipe, and six little pairs of legs went scampering upstairs. Tim hesitated a minute, not daring to ask whether he ought to go too, finally decided he had better, and went nervously last.

'Here the last shall go. Hulloa, stop a bit; you're new, ain't you? You needn't come, you know, for your first fortnight; when you've been here longer you won't be in such a hurry to fag,' and Tim retired very red, among the titters of the other little wretches. He gave a start as on entering his room he perceived Weston apparently glued to the wall behind the door. 'Hush! hold your tongue, Skinny,' said that young gentleman in a hoarse whisper; then having peeped through the crack of the door, he added in his usual tones, 'It's all right; he's sent Sawnders; rough luck on the beggar, but he's rather a scalliwag, so I don't care; besides he's fat, and the exercise will do him good; he'd take the prize over you any day.' and with a valedictory punch in the ribs to his host, delivered apparently with a view to ascertaining the amount of flesh there, and followed by an elaborate pantomime of having hurt his knuckles, he slid down the banisters and vanished.

Thus Ebbesley, as he was now to be called, began to be aware of the fact that Eton, besides being the dwelling-place of Carol, contained some 898 other boys, of ages varying from his own to twenty years, whose existence he had in his day-dreams completely ignored, a course by no means open to him when brought into actual contact with those young gentlemen. Not that any one meant to be particularly unkind to him, but he was such a forlorn-looking little creature, his high hat was so big for him, and his fingers so inky, that it seemed somehow natural and handy to launch a casual kick or slighting remark at him in passing, — greetings bestowed almost unconsciously, and which would never have affected a more robust temperament, but which the poor child took as indications of a deep-seated ill-will towards him on the part of his schoolfellows. It was all part of the tendency to take things hard, predicted in old days by the wise old doctor at Stoke Ashton. He felt an atmosphere of hostility, and froze under it, becoming very silent and rather sulky, by no means a happy course for conciliating schoolboys. Carol with frank boyish manners, good looks, an inborn knack of games, and the experience of a private school, had soon found his level, and having punched the head of Swamp minor for calling him 'Miss Darling' on account of his fair skin, had established a footing in the semi-barbarous community, to which only the strong can attain; whereas Tim, unused to the society of boys, forbidden by the doctor to play violent games on account of his health, too weak to withstand bullying, yet too simple-minded to lie or cringe, the natural weapons of the otherwise defenceless, was like a person who had been long kept in a dark and silent room, suddenly exposed in some busy thoroughfare to the full glare of the noonday sun; he was dazed by the fulness of life that surged around him. That very quality which seems so full of beauty to sentimental people like Mr. Gray (with whose works, containing the celebrated ode to Eton College, the head-master presents the students on their leaving), and which another poet of our own day has described in the lines at the head of this chapter as 'all this stir and rout,' was sufficiently bewildering to our little country boy set suddenly down in the midst of it. We who look back on school-life through the softening haze of memory, forget that the boys so perfectly satisfactory from an aesthetic point of view have ceased to have the power of inflicting pain upon us, while they possess it in an astonishing degree in the case of their schoolfellows. Luckily for our hero, active corporeal bullying had gone out of fashion before his day, but small boys possess the art of wounding by words and looks in a perfection quite unknown to the other sex in any stage of development, and when they give their minds to it can make a sensitive companion's life as thorough a burthen to him as need be wished. You, dear lady, who read this, if you know any little boys at school near you who have left home for the first time, ask leave for the poor little souls to come out and spend the day with you. Don't stop to think that they will find it dull, that you are not used to boys and shan't know how to amuse them; they won't need amusing. It will be happiness enough to get away from school and into a home for an hour or two. Take the little red hands in your delicate palm and ask kind questions about home and family; you will be doing a really charitable thing, and will win a mother's gratitude when the next Sunday letter is written; or if your little visitor have no mother, Heaven help him, he needs all your goodness ten times the more. But don't ask the elder boys; they would rather play cricket, and won't say thank you.

If Tim shed a few tears in his turn-up bedstead sometimes, in the silence of the night, no one was aware of the fact but that remarkable piece of furniture, whose venerable timbers must have absorbed too much of that form of moisture, first and last, to have looked on it as a novelty. He had no loving mother, poor soul, to whom to unburthen his grief in long incoherent letters; he would not unnecessarily distress Mrs. Quitchett, and of his father he was too much in awe to dare to complain to him of anything at Eton, after his eagerness to be allowed to go there. To the world at large—or rather at small, if the coining of such an expression is permissible, for his public was a very limited one—he was simply a specimen of a very common form of scug, whom exclusion from the citizenship of games had degraded into a helotry, which translated itself to the outward eye principally by ink and a tendency to loaf up town and look into shop-windows, the High Street being built in a straight line with the College, and to walk up it requiring consequently less active volition than to go in any other direction. It was this tendency to follow his nose, coupled with his love of animals, that caused many of his walks to end in the back-yard of a rather dingy little shop where ferrets, canary-birds, rabbits, and such small game, formed the stock-in-trade of the dirtiest old man Tim had ever seen. He was one day watching the attempts of six little birds with red beaks to attain to freedom of action in a cage where one of them would have been rather cramped for room, when the proprietor of the establishment invited him in.

'Wouldn't yer like to take a look round the premises, sir? No need to buy nothing yer don't want. Alway glad of inspection. I've some remarkable nice young rats, if they was at all in your line, and a beautiful little terrier bitch I should like to show yer as a pictur, not with any notion of selling.'

So Tim took a look round the 'premisses,' saw the baby rats like little lumps of raw beef squeaking round their sharp-nosed, bright-eyed parent, the wicked-looking lithe ferrets, the ridiculous fancy pigeons, the stolidly munching lop-eared rabbits, and the 'beautiful little terrier bitch,' a shivering, forlorn little mongrel, who was howling dismally in a superannuated tub. A certain air of mouldy dejection seemed common to all the denizens of this remarkable yard, in marked contrast to the shop, where a dozen canaries were all piping and shrilling fit to burst their swollen little yellow throats. Tim bought some rabbits, no doubt at considerably more than their market value, but which were cheap to him as giving him an interest in life, and a vested right to visit this charming emporium at his own discretion. The owner of the establishment made a handsome income out of the board and lodging of those rabbits, but a really enterprising man is never content when on the track of a good thing, and his efforts to dispose of other inmates of the yard to his customer on similarly advantageous terms were as unflagging as they were fruitless.

'Yer see this 'ere ferret, sir,' he would say; 'he *is* a beauty now. I shall sell 'im to young Lord Ratisbane as boards at the Rev. — 's; 'is lordship'll give me whatever I like to ask 'im for sich a ferret as that, once he gets his eyes on 'im,' and so forth; but Tim remained undazzled. He possessed a fund of quiet obstinacy, and he did not like ferrets; fancy prices given by youthful members of the aristocracy had little empire over his imagination. But temptation takes many forms, and this old man was as subtile as the Scriptural serpent in his adjustment of his lures to the special character with which he had to deal. Finding Tim's mind not set in the direction of sport, he plied him with pets of a more domestic nature; a tortoise of the most fascinating ugliness was offered him on terms which he was assured were exceptionally advantageous.

'I don't want to over-persuade yer, sir, I'm sure, but if you fancies tortoises, why yer couldn't 'ave a nicer one.'

The tortoise which the old man balanced on the palm of one extended hand, while with the other he thoughtfully stroked a tame rat that was ascending his shoulder, protruded its cross face and hissed at Tim with deadly malignity, then it withdrew permanently into its shell.

'I'm sure it's a very nice tortoise, if one happened to want one,' the customer said, with his usual grave politeness; 'but you see I have the rabbits to come and see here, and I don't think the tortoise would be happy in my room —'

'In yer room, is it?' burst in the dirty old man; 'if you'd 'a mentioned it sooner, I'd 'a told yer as I 'ad the very thing yer wanted. If it's a 'ouse pet ye're in want of, what *can* be nicer than a good canary?'

'It wouldn't do,' said Tim; 'some big fellows made Biggies get rid of his; they said it disturbed them when they wanted to do their verses.'

'Why, if *that's* all!' cried the irrepressible, 'as sure as my name's Skelton, the thing for you is dormice: *they* don't sing now, do they?' he added, with engaging humour; 'they won't disturb no one's verses now, they won't.'

There was no resisting the dormice. As Mr. Skelton fished the little balls of soft fur out of the hay in an old cigar-box, barred across the top with some bits of wire, Tim's heart went out to them. There and then the bargain was completed, and Mr. Skelton chuckled as he jingled the coin transferred in the transaction, in his black and horny palm.

'That's a rum little lot,' he remarked reflectively, as he watched the little figure balancing the big hat trotting down the sunny street with its new possession. 'Most on 'em, they comes in and they turns the place upside down, and they lets out the rats, and pokes the ferrets; and it's "Skelton, what's this?" and "Skelton, 'ere," and "Skelton, there," and "Quick, please, I'm in a 'urry," — they're always in a 'urry. But this one, 'e's as sober and old-fashioned as a little judge, and 'e argifies and explains, and 'e says "No, thank you," and he pays 'is money too: ah! and 'e won't go on tick neither; 'e ain't like most on 'em.'

The subject of this character-study had meanwhile been visited by a sudden thought, which he was inclined to regard almost as an inspiration. He felt with painful acuteness the barrier that had sprung up between himself and Carol. Their relations were as different from what he had hoped as they well could be. The most elementary knowledge of school-life would have shown him that this was inevitable. But knowledge of life, school or otherwise, was just what Tim was farthest from possessing. He remembered Carol's fondness for his squirrel and for all animals; he knew that they could not be companions and friends as he had dreamed that they might, but surely it was in his power to make Carol think of him sometimes. He thought over his plan carefully on all sides, and by the time he reached his tutor's, had come to the conclusion that there could be nothing against it.

When Carol came in to change before dinner, he was not a little astonished to find on his table a little cage fitted up with a sort of treadmill, and containing two dormice fast asleep in a handful of hay. He searched in vain for any superscription that might explain this eccentric gift, and finally came to the conclusion it must be a joke of some of his friends. Several of his intimates were summoned, but denied all knowledge of the affair.

'It must be that brute the hyena,' said Villidge minor. 'It's just the sort of thing he'd think funny.'

But the youth known to his associates as the hyena because, as the matron expressed it, he was 'prone to risibility,' protested, on being appealed to, that he was as innocent as the rest.

'If Curly has an unknown admirer whose tribute takes the form of the smaller varieties of mammalia, I don't see why *I* should be held responsible.'

At dinner Darley's mysterious present was the great topic and joke of the top table. Carol bore all the bantering good-naturedly, but after a good deal of it began to feel a little put out. To be the object of a joke was a new position to him, and he didn't like it. He had a perfect gathering in his room after two, to look at the wretched little animals, slumbering peacefully through all the disturbance they were creating. It being apparently impossible to discover who had put this affront upon him, the next question was how to get rid of the creatures. To keep dormice like a scug of a lower boy was of course out of the question.

Meanwhile no echoes of the mirth in the upper circles of the house penetrated as far down in the social scale as Tim, who was serenely pluming himself on his tact and discretion. He had debated at first what would be the right thing to write with this present, and had at last solved the difficulty by depositing the offering anonymously. 'He will guess whom they are from,' he thought; 'no one else would think of such a thing, or knows how he cares for animals; he will say something at fagging-time.' For Carol had fulfilled his promise of taking Tim for his fag, explaining the apparent eccentricity of his choice to the expostulating Villidge major, who was captain of the house, by saying that he 'knew him at home.' and that fifteen minutes of bondage, at which most of the small boys muttered and grumbled, became to 'Ebbesley' the happiest time of the day, for then he was sure of a smile and a kind word, and each piece of toast made for his hero's consumption became a labour of love; he scorched his face and burnt his fingers with perfect equanimity, and thought scorn of Biggies, whom he once detected doing his master's toast at the gas. On this particular evening, however, when he appeared as usual, Carol seemed preoccupied, and rather sulky; he only said, 'Let's see, have you made your three bits, and the tea? All right, there's nothing else; you can go.'

Tim made some excuse to loiter a minute or two, apparently busy at the cupboard, and hazarded a furtive glance round the room in search of his present. The little cage was reposing on the top of the bed, jammed in between a big Liddell and Scott and some fives gloves, where it had been stuck by the maid when she cleared the table for tea. Just then Carol's messmate arrived, accompanied by his fag, and plunged anew into the topic of the day.

'Well, Curly; found out who sent the dormice?'

Carol answered with what was for him to display considerable irritation,' I wish to goodness I could; I'd give the fellow as good a kicking as ever he had in his life.'

'Well, I can dispose of 'em for you any way; here's Weston will take 'em off your hands and ask no questions.' And giving the cage and its inmates to his fag, he added, laughing, 'There, it's an ill wind that blows no one good; I'm sure you've been dying for some dormice all the half, haven't you, Weston? and I know you never keep any money after the first week.'

Tommy, astonished but nothing loth, carried off his booty grinning; and Tim, who till then had not trusted himself to look round, got out of the room as best he could. In the passage he found his brother fag pausing to examine his treasures.

'Hulloa, Skinny!' he exclaimed, as Tim drew near, 'here's a queer go: what on earth should make Darley give me a couple of dormice? I went in expecting to get pulled for burning the toast, and see what I get instead of a pitching into.'

Tim had got under a gas-lamp, so that his face was black and invisible, but when he tried to speak, Tommy looked up suddenly.

'Why, you're blubbing,' he said; 'whatever's the matter?'

For all answer Ebbesley darted into his own room, which was not far distant, whither, with mingled curiosity and alarm, the other followed him.

'What's up?' he asked, not unsympathetically; and Tim, feeling he must tell some one, sobbed out—

'Oh! Weston, it was me who got the dormice, and I thought he'd like them; you know I knew him at home, and he used to have a squirrel; I forgot it was some time ago—and—and—' but Tommy had collapsed into the one chair and was shaking with laughter; the exquisite humour of the whole affair was altogether too much for him.

'Oh, don't, please don't!' cried Tim, to whom the matter was deadly serious. 'If Carol should hear, he'd be angry with me; you heard what he said, and I meant to please him.'

'What did you call him?' cried Weston. '"Carol"! What a name! Oh, don't I just wish I was a little bigger or he a little lower down; wouldn't I chaff him. We've always wanted to know his name; most fellows thought it was only Charles or something, but I knew it was something outlandish, because he always had "C. Darley" on his letters, and took such pains never to let it out.'

'Oh dear!' said poor Tim, 'I seem to be always doing the wrong thing; please don't say anything about it; he wouldn't like it—and I couldn't bear him to be angry with me.'

'What a baby it is,' thought Weston, looking down at the tear-stained imploring face before him.

'But you'll keep the secret,' urged Tim despairingly; 'never tell any one about the dormice.'

Something in his utter childishness touched the softer side of Tommy's callous little-boy's heart.

'Yes, I promise,' he said; and he kept his word.

'I say, you know,' he said next day to Tim, meeting him in one of the passages, 'I've been thinking, Skinny, those dormice are really yours, you know; you ought to have them.'

'Oh no, no!' cried poor Skinny vehemently, 'I never want to see them again; and — and — thank you always for keeping the secret.'

So Tommy kept both the secret and the dormice until, once going home ill for a week, and leaving no directions as to their nourishment, he found on his return that one of them had succumbed to this prolonged fast, which so distressed him that he made over the cage and the survivor to a friend.

But the fates were busy with those dormice. His new possessor, thinking that a little sunshine would be good for the shattered constitution of the widower, left him on the window-sill when he went to school, and whether it was the wind, the boys' maid, or the matron's cat, was never known; but on his return the little cage lay broken in the street, and the last of his race was embarked on a sleep such as even he had never compassed in this world.

CHAPTER VI

How far too sweet for school he seemed to me;
How ripe for combat with the wits of men;
How childlike in his manhood.
— *Ionica, II,*

It must not be supposed that life was uniformly dark to Tim in these early days at Eton. He had sources of happiness quite distinct from his glimpses of Carol, which had certainly turned out less satisfactory than his hopes. After the dormice episode he was shyer and more constrained in the presence of his fag-master than ever. But he had found and always kept a marvellously kind understanding and tender friend in his tutor, whose manly gentle soul went forth to this forlorn little specimen of suffering humanity; he readily guessed that the path of such a baby could not but be thorny, and though he was necessarily obliged, for many reasons, to ignore much of what he knew, and the whole of what he suspected, he managed in a hundred small ways to soften the existence of the youngest and dreariest of his pupils. If I do not say much of Tim's Eton tutor, and the large part he filled in his history, it is because, while among several thousand boys who have passed through the school in the last twenty years, to describe two or three is fairly safe, it were quite otherwise to draw anything like an accurate picture of one of the comparatively few men who have filled the post of tutor there during the same period. So I may only note in passing the fact of his untiring and thoughtful kindness, and the grateful affection it elicited in return. His study was a haven of refuge to Tim on many a rainy after-four, while the employment said by Dr. Watts to be provided for that class of member was busily occupying numerous pairs of idle hands in other parts of the house. There or on the banks of the kind old river in the shady playing-fields he spent long happy hours with Scott or Shakespeare for companion. Mr. Ebbesley was liberal in the matter of pocket-money, and as Tim's tastes were not as a rule expensive, he was able to revel in delightful books. Had his examinations been in authors of his own selection I have no doubt he would have attained the highest honours.

Another favourite resort of his was the old chapel in the Castle at Windsor: the grand quiet of the place, with its dim, coloured light and ghostly armorial flags ranged overhead, soothed and comforted him after many a bitter childish trial; but the highest pleasure came from the pealing organ and the pure true voices of one of the best of English choirs. To Tim, whose soul was full of melody, but whose only experience of sacred music had been the not very perfect performances in the village church at home, the grand outbursts of song which the great musicians had given from their hearts to the worship of God, were as waters in the desert. The first time he heard the beautiful prayer that Mendelssohn has wedded to immortal music, the yearning for doves' wings to fly away and be at rest, rendered by a fresh boy's voice, the tears gathered in his eyes, and he forgot where he was, standing wrapped in an ecstasy, his soul afloat on the wings of the music. It seemed to him as if he and this other boy no older than himself were somehow one, that the pearly notes he was listening to did not come from the shiny emotionless little chorister whose mouth was moving, but from the inmost depths of his own heart.

Tim could not really sing a note, though he would dearly have liked to; but he often had this feeling afterwards, in the following winter, when he joined the musical society and used to sit silent and happy between two deep-lunged little monsters, and have all the sensation of pouring forth his being in song. Carol, who had a lusty baritone, and a fondness for music of the more robust and cheerful order, having been ordered to recruit trebles at his tutor's, and finding the lower boys for the most part unwilling to display their accomplishments, had had recourse in despair to his fag, who was of course enchanted with the prospect.

'I'm afraid I shan't be much use, but I should like to come,' he said modestly, and come he did with exemplary punctuality.

His relations with his contemporaries were still, for the most part, lacking in cordiality. He had no gift of making himself known to them, and they were not sufficiently interested in him to take trouble in getting to know him. The discovery at the beginning of the Michaelmas half that he was forbidden to play football, set the finishing touch to the contempt his house-fellows were inclined to entertain for him, and except in school or at the musical society he came in contact with no boys but such as boarded at his tutor's. There was one youth, however, who, contrary to all likelihood, took a desultory interest in Tim, and that was Tommy Weston. The episode of the dormice had disclosed to Tommy certain things about Tim that lay outside the range of his daily observation of life and character, and being of an inquiring turn of mind, he determined to frequent this new specimen of boy, taking at first a purely analytic and microscopic view of him, with which, as the weeks went by, something of a kindlier and more human sentiment began to mingle. I don't know what has become of Tommy Weston since, but in those days he promised to be a very remarkable man. He possessed indomitable tenacity and strength of purpose, coupled with a mercurial gaiety of temperament, endless patience, entire disregard of public opinion, immense courage, a keen sense of the ridiculous, and a composure and self-possession on which the most trying circumstances were powerless to produce any effect. To Tim he was a most marvellous outcome. At first the little boy was rather alarmed by this remarkable phenomenon, though humbly grateful for his attentions, but by degrees he came to be more at home with him, and Tommy was the only person to whom he ever confided some part of his feeling for Carol; only a very little and in moments of rare expansion, for Tommy was not sentimental, and regarded subjective conversation as more or less profitless. But the shy revelations of character made by Tim struck him, as I have said, as a 'queer start,' and as such were regarded by him with a wonder which that youth was glad to mistake for sympathy. 'It is certainly not on the principle of Mary and the lamb.' he said to himself, 'that Skinny's partiality can be explained, for Darley don't "love the lamb, you know." Fancy Skinny wandering into tutor's upper set at private, and Villidge and all of 'em hollering out in pupil-room, "What makes the lamb love Curly so?"' and he was so tickled by the weirdness of this notion that he accosted Tim as 'lambkin' next time he saw him, and chuckled to himself, remarking generally, 'What rot nursery rhymes were,' in a manner calculated to mystify that simple-minded young person. Indeed, he was in such high good-humour that he invited him into his room, an apartment decorated with all manner of ingenious inventions from designs of Tommy's own; such as an elaborate apparatus in which the poker was involved for shutting the window without leaving bed, and another by which water was discharged on any assailant who might attempt to turn the sleeping inhabitant up in that piece of furniture. This last machine, which was constructed with much ingenuity out of a bandbox, a broken jug, seven yards of twine, the leg of one of his chairs (propped, in the absence of its limb, on his hat-box), and the cover of his Gradus, was subsequently destroyed by his tutor, after deluging the matron (Tommy swore accidentally), who was coming to administer medicine when he stayed out in collection-week. These and similar treasures were displayed to the wondering eyes of Skinny, as well as a cardboard box in which he kept the prime fetishes of his worship; his name, which it is hardly necessary to mention was not Tommy, and the date of his birth, written very neatly in his own blood, a sheet of broad rule completely covered with a design in concentric and intersecting circles, of which the object did not distinctly appear, and another, on which he had jotted down the numbers of all the cabs he had ever ridden in, on his rare visits to the metropolis, and reduced the added result, by some process inscrutable by the unmathematical mind, to pounds, shillings, and pence.

Now it happened one Sunday in the Lent term when the flats around Eton were swept by a relentless east wind, that Tommy had agreed with a kindred soul from another house to go with him to the Ditton woods and gather primroses; not that the 'primrose by the river's brim' was anything more to either of them than the yellow primrose it was to the gentleman in the poem, but it lent an object to their walk, and a delicious flavour of the illegal in the combined facts that they would trespass, and very probably be late for lock-up, which in those days, when chapel was at three, closed the period of Sunday afternoon leisure. Whether Tommy's friend was detected talking in chapel and made to stay at home and do his Sunday questions, or merely turned lazy and preferred to read a book by the fire, I have no means of deciding with certainty; but the fact remains that he threw Tommy over when it was too late to make other arrangements, to the no small disgust of Master Weston, who was not fond of abandoning any enterprise he had once formed. In these straits he bethought him of Tim, who was quite sure to have no engagement, and went in search of him. Tim was writing his weekly letter to his father, but consented readily to accompany him, if he would wait till he had finished; and the concluding sentences were rendered even more laborious than usual to the scribe, by the distracting behaviour of his companion, who was occupying the interval with a sort of highland fling, while he sang to a well-known Scottish air, just then familiarised to Southern ears by the base uses of a comic song, these remarkable words —

Oh, Jerusalem, Jerusalem, Jerusalem,
Oh, Jerusalem, the costermonger's donkey.

'Oh! please, Tommy, don't make that dreadful noise,' said poor Tim. 'How can I get done?'

'Dreadful noise, indeed! it's a Sabbath hymn, you profane little wretch,' retorted the irrepressible, at the same time pulling Tim's inky pen upwards through his fingers, to teach him, as he said, proper respect to his elders.

At length the epistle was concluded, and when Tommy had stuck the stamps on wrong side up in the bottom left-hand corner (which called forth a severe little lecture on slovenly ways in Tim's next letter from home) they started on their walk. Through the College and playing-fields all went well, but once in the open fields beyond, their progress was considerably retarded by various skirmishes with the class magnificently lumped together by the boys, in their sublime innocent snobbishness, as 'cads,' and including the sons of all tradesmen, farmers, and the labouring classes generally, who happened to inhabit the neighbourhood. There was not a 'cad' within miles with whom Tommy was not on intimate terms; he knew the Christian names, pursuits, and family history of every old man or woman who drove into Eton for purposes of trade and barter, the commodities in which they dealt, and the days when they might be expected. There was one elderly lady whom he addressed as Sarah, and to whom he invariably offered marriage, regardless of the fact that she was a matron of many years' standing; and an old man in a red waistcoat, who had business relations with some one in the town, would hang about for hours watching for an opportunity to slip unnoticed past the window from which this awful boy had a torrent of ever-varying chaff and nicknames ready to pour out upon him on all occasions. With the rising generation of cad-dom, the lads of his own age or a little older, his relations were, however, by no means so friendly. He had fought with nearly all, and licked most; and on the few Herculean youths who had succeeded in forcing him to beat a retreat his vengeance had subsequently descended, when their evil stars led them to pass his dwelling, in the form of coals, sugar, earth from his flower-box, or the inside round of paper off the tops of raspberry jam; sometimes the pot itself, if nearly empty of its succulent contents, would startle the echoes of a dark night as it crashed to ruin against the palings of the opposite house, while a muttered curse succeeded the jaunty whistling of the passing victim.

The two boys were crossing a ploughed field where the ridges on which they stepped crumbled beneath their feet, dry and powdery under the March wind, when they encountered a detachment of small boys of the class described above, headed by a youth a few years older than the rest, who wore his hat on one side in a raffish manner, calculated to provoke remark. Tommy inquired politely if it was stuck on with glue, or how otherwise it retained its position.

'Just you 'old *your* row, young Weston.' retorted the insulted party; 'I knows you'; thus implying some mysterious secret hold over Tommy, which that youth was hasty to repudiate.

'Take care not to come too close,' he replied with studied moderation, 'or I *may* hurt you.'

'What, *you*? You're too young and too small; 'it one o' your own size,' said the champion, and all the satellites applauded.

Tommy, feeling the moment for decisive action had arrived, made a threatening advance, whereupon the small fry scattered and fled; and their leader, seeing himself abandoned by his myrmidons, also retired, but in good order, and still hurling taunts, which increased in bitterness in proportion as the chances of pursuit seemed to grow less. Tim, I need not say, was made very unhappy by this sort of encounter; and what with these numerous delays and the fact that they had started late for their walk, the brief afternoon was already far spent when they arrived at the paling they must climb to enter the Park. Tim pulled out his watch and looked at it doubtfully.

'We haven't *more* than time to get home before lock-up,' he said.

'Well?' inquired Tommy, who was already astride upon the paling, as though Tim had started some question entirely foreign to the matter in hand.

'If we go on, we shall be late,' persisted Tim.

'Oh! is *that* all?' said Tommy, who had a sublime contempt for law when it interfered in any way with what he proposed to himself to do. As I have said, the primroses were less than nothing to him, but having started to pick primroses, primroses he would pick, and a lion in the path would not have deterred him for a moment. Now Tim had, on the contrary, profound respect for law and order, and if he unwittingly transgressed the most formal of little school-rules, felt unhappy and criminal for days afterwards.

'I think I shall go back,' he said after a pause.

'You may do as you please,' said his companion; '*I'm* going to get primroses,' and therewith he slid down on the other side of the paling and was lost to view. 'Are you coming?' he shouted back.

Tim still stood irresolute: he was alone. Tommy having vanished, it seemed easier to withstand his influence than when under that cold eye from the top of the fence. He was cold; he did not want to be out late; he did not want to get a pœna; above all, he did not want to shirk fagging.

'I shall go back,' he persisted, and he went.

'Give my love to tutor.' Tommy called from within, 'and tell him not to worry about me; I shall most likely be back for early school to-morrow.'

Tim had a dreary walk homewards; the wind, which had before been with them, was now in his face, and he had to butt at it, head down, and hands deep in his trouser-pockets. Discomforts became prominent which had before only made a scarcely noticed background to Tommy's enlivening conversation, and the somewhat perilous excitement of his passages of wit with the passers-by. Tim began to wonder vaguely, not without terror, whether he would fall into any of the wasps' nests that his companion had so successfully stirred up as they came along. Visions of angry cads, still smarting with a sense of unavenged insults, flitted through his uneasy mind, and caused him to hug the hedgerows rather than launch across the bare fields, where his figure would be a more conspicuous object. He tried to determine on a course of action in case of attack. Tommy, he had observed, advanced boldly in such cases, assumed the aggressive attitude, and the assailants fled; it seemed to him a fresh proof of the unsatisfactoriness with which matters were arranged in this world, that the people who seemed to possess the knack of coming scot-free out of awkward situations were precisely those to whom it was of least importance to do so. Something told him that it would be in vain for *him* to attempt the same line as Tommy; some irresolution or faltering at the last minute would be sure to betray him, and his assumed boldness would only make his position the less pleasant. The conviction was forced in upon him that to make your antagonist unwilling to fight, *you* must be genuinely anxious to do so. 'And in *that* case,' reasoned he, 'there would be no pleasure, but the reverse, in seeing the other fellow sheer off.' All of which seemed to him mysterious and unkind. 'It would surely have been as easy to settle human nature on a plan that should enable each individual to obtain what he wanted.' Nor were his apprehensions altogether groundless.

As he passed along one of the leafless hedges a hard object whizzed by him, and rattled on the frozen turf beside him; there was little or no doubt it was a stone. Through the hedge, which was thick and tangled, though the leaves were off, he could dimly detect moving forms and smothered laughter. He tried to persuade himself that the thrower had only aimed at something in the hedge, and that if he kept quiet they would pass on without noticing him; so he crouched down as close to the bank as possible, and kept very still.

I am compelled as a truthful biographer to admit that physical courage was not a characteristic of my hero, and as he held his breath in the undignified attitude he had assumed, he could hear his heart beat loud with apprehension. There was a pause, and then a muttered conference, and presently another stone followed the first. Placed as he was, Tim was pretty safe, and two or three succeeding missiles passed innocently over him. Then came another pause; the attacking party were surprised that no attempt was made to return fire, and they feared an ambush.

The fact was that he of the hat had joined forces with some other lads of his own size, discarding the crew of weaklings who had deserted him in his hour of need, and they had taken up a position in which to waylay Tommy on his return to Eton, and seize an unique opportunity of wiping off old scores by humiliating their enemy without doing him any great injury. It is only fair to them to state that there is no good ground for supposing that they deliberately attacked Tim knowing him to be alone; they probably thought his warlike friend was with him, and the stones were only meant to open the affair, and force Tommy to disclose himself. Having debated among themselves, they could think of no better plan than to fire another volley, which they accordingly did, and Tim had closed his eyes and given himself up for lost when he heard unmistakable signs of terror and confusion behind the hedge, and then the sound of a general stampede of hastily retreating footsteps.

The next minute some one cleared the hedge and alighted close to him, and a well-known voice exclaimed, 'The brutes! they were rocking a little fellow; I wish to goodness I'd caught one of them. Hullo! Ebbesley, is that you? Why, how the deuce did *you* get into this sort of row?'

Tim hardly yet realised that it was Carol who had dropped, as it were, out of the gray sky for his deliverance, and who now stood before him, with cheeks flushed by wind and running, holding out large kind hands to pull him on to his feet again. He felt relieved and grateful, and yet somewhat ashamed of the position in which he had been discovered, and began hastily to explain —

'I had gone to walk with Weston, and he said something to that fellow, and he didn't like it, and Weston went after him, and he ran away; and then we separated, because I wanted to get back —'

'And our friend meanwhile conceived the brilliant plan of lying in wait for you, and shying stones at you from behind a hedge. What distinguished bravery!' interrupted Villidge minor, who had been with Carol, and who now joined the party through an adjacent gap.

'What an infernal coward!' cried Darley, whose eyes flashed with martial ardour.

'He is, luckily for him, beyond the reach of chastisement for the present,' rejoined the more phlegmatic Villidge; 'though I flatter myself that a well-directed pebble was not altogether without effect on the calf of his leg. You'd better cut home, Ebbesley, if you want to be in time for lock-up, and thank your stars Darley and I happened to come along when we did,' Tim would have liked to thank them, but found no words, so trotted off as fast as his legs would carry him.

'It's just as I thought, Curly,' continued Villidge, as he and Carol followed at a more leisurely pace; 'it's that little monster Weston who has brought your unhappy fag into the scrape in which we found him. I saw them together the other day, and reflected that collapse must sooner or later be the fate of such a frail little vessel in the same stream with such an iron pot as Master Tommy.'

But Carol did not at once answer; he was watching the queer little figure scudding along in front of them, and the sight of that small form buffeted by the bitter weather somehow suggested to him how unfit such a creature must be to fight his way through the rough places of lower-boy life.

'Do you remember,' Villidge continued, also looking at Tim, 'how much exercised you were when Ebbesley first came as to what you could do for him, in the way of looking after him, and that sort of thing? I'm thinking that this piece of knight-errantry of yours in his behalf comes most happily to solve the difficulty; you could hardly have done him a better turn, or looked after him to more purpose than by snatching him from the fate of the first martyr.'

'There's not much knight-what's-his-name in having a lot of lubberly beasts run away when you look at 'em,' replied Carol modestly. 'Seriously though, it had just occurred to me that perhaps I hadn't done all I might have to make that poor little fellow's life easy to him.'

'I can't see that it is incumbent on you to act dry-nurse to all my tutor's scugs; you might keep a piece of pumice-stone in your room to take the ink off their grimy little hands, or save up the rough copies of your verses to stuff your young friend's hat, and keep it a hair's-breadth or two higher above his ears, but I really don't see what else you could do for him.'

'Don't you think such a boy as that must be rather bullied among the small fellows?'

'Oh! I daresay not a bit more than is good for him; and besides, if Tommy's taken him up he'll be all right; for though he'll probably land him in rows with the beaks, he's an oracle among the lower boys, and if he says he's a good sort, they'll all discover they always said so. So don't make yourself unhappy about him.'

And as Carol was not fond of making himself unhappy, he took the advice.

CHAPTER VII

Happy places have grown holy;
If we went where once we went,
Only tears would fall down slowly
As at solemn sacrament.

Mrs. Browning.

It is not my intention to trace in detail Tim's career at school, which, after all, presents few points of interest. His first two years were certainly not a period of unmixed enjoyment; but other boys before and after him have gone through much the same experience without taking much harm from it. And after a time boys get tired of persecution, as of other pursuits. It is not worth their while to continue to bully, unless there is some special reason for it, and in Tim's case there was none; his offences were all purely negative, sins of omission, absence of qualities decreed to be necessary to salvation by the *Vehm-gericht* of collective boyhood through many generations.

Villidge was right to a certain extent in his prophecy of the good effects likely to spring from the patronage of Tommy. There is little or no doubt that Tim's ultimate admission to a recognised social standing owed its first small beginnings to his intimacy with that eccentric youth. Boys go in flocks; and if it is the fashion to treat one of their number with unkindness, while the active throw each his little stone, the passive turn aside and stop their ears to the victim's groans. We are not all thieves, and are in the habit of returning thanks for that fact, but when a fellow-traveller has fallen in with a band of these gentry, the proportion of Samaritans to priests and Levites is not large, and nowhere smaller than among boys. But when the tide turns, and some one with more character than the rest picks up the wounded comrade and gives him a word of encouragement, pronouncing him 'not such a very bad lot,' the rest veer round, and peace is restored. It is impossible to fix the exact date of the change; the deliverance is as intangible as the persecution. To Tim it came far more slowly than Villidge, with his happy knack of establishing coincidence between his wishes and probability, had foretold for the comfort of Darley's uneasy conscience.

It is true that Weston was popular among his contemporaries, but at the time of the Ditton expedition he was still in Fourth Form, and the

Remove little boys, though they frequented him freely and to a certain extent admired him, would not have accepted his opinion of a third person where it differed in any way from their own. But a young man who had been for almost two years in Fifth Form could not be expected to recollect these subtle distinctions of lower-boy life.

The leaven was working surely, however. Tommy stuck staunchly to his protégé, as they mounted the lowest rungs in the ladder together, and by Tim's third summer-half, when he had been two years at Eton, had learnt to keep his fingers freer from ink, and to wear hats that fitted him, he stood firmly on a platform from which he could look back with tolerable equanimity on his past troubles. This half Fifth Form would open its portals to him, and he would cease to be a lower boy; but, alas! this was also Carol's last half at school, and little as had come of his dreamed-of companionship, that was a thought on which Tim could hardly trust himself to dwell. He had made a few little acquaintanceships since it had become the fashion to find good in him, and was no longer desolate, but he did not make friends readily, and these new connections with the world around him left quite untouched the old ruling devotion of his life whose roots were very deep in him indeed. Carol was almost more his hero than ever. The very separateness of their respective positions served to enhance his devotion. It seemed quite right and natural that Carol should be a king among men, should stand at the corner of the street with other godlike beings, his peers—yet how immeasurably below him in the estimation of his faithful admirer—should carry a cane (badge of the greatest honour!) at football matches in the winter, and play cricket for the eleven in summer. His walls were decorated with caps of many colours—the eleven, the 'Field,' the house cap, and many more. Pewter cups won in athletic contests occupied little carved brackets over his chimney-piece, and the rules of 'Pop' framed in pale blue ribbon sprawled over half the available space on one side of his little room. In short, he was the typical 'swell' or successful public-school boy, and a very kindly, gentle, magnanimous fellow into the bargain, as became his greatness.

Tim used to trot off to the playing-fields in those long hot days, and lie there under the trees, watching the light athletic figure clad in white flannel springing hither and thither in the game, till the other boys, knowing his indifference to their sports, wondered sometimes at the regularity of his attendance at all the cricket matches.

It was Saturday after-twelve, and Tim was occupying his usual corner, with his rug spread on the edge of the shadow, and a half-eaten bag of cherries beside him. The first innings was just over, and Carol, released from his duties in the field, came sauntering round the ground arm-in-arm with another magnificent young cricketer like himself. Tim was turning his attention, no longer claimed by the game, to the firm red fruit, when he heard his name spoken in the voice that never failed to make his nerves thrill.

'Hulloa, Ebbesley!' said his lord and fag-master loftily, but not unkindly, 'what are you up to? Wasting your time as usual, eh?'

'I was looking at you.' answered the little boy simply and truthfully, wholly unaware that his reply partook of the nature of repartee. Carol flushed and looked a little annoyed; then he laughed.

'That's one for me, anyhow,' he said, as he resumed his walk.

'Who's your young friend?' asked his companion.

'My fag; he's one of the queerest little beggars I ever saw; I know him at home, and am supposed to look after him. I've been trying for two years to discover the meaning of the term, and the duties connected with it.'

'You've some cheek, answering Darley like that,' said the stout Sawnders, who, too lazy to bring down a rug, and having neither money nor credit wherewith to obtain cherries, had decided to bestow his company on Tim in return for a share of those luxuries.

'I didn't mean to be cheeky,' said Tim, aghast; 'do you suppose he was angry?'

'I don't believe he half liked it, before another swell; he got very red.'

'Oh dear me!' said Tim wearily, 'I seem always to say the wrong thing.'

'Well, you'd better come back to my tutor's now, anyway,' said Sawnders; 'it's a quarter to two, and they won't begin the next innings before dinner.'

As they went towards College, Tim, whose mind was busy with the thought that he had offended Carol, felt himself taken by the scruff of the neck, and turning to expostulate, found himself in the grasp of his tutor, who regarded him with keen friendly eyes. 'Well, little boy,' he said, 'have you been looking at the match?'

'Yes, sir.'

'All after twelve?'

'Yes, sir.'

'And you mean to come back after four?'

'Yes, I think so, sir.'

'Have you done all your work?'

'Yes, sir.'

'Then I think you had much better come out with me. You don't care a rap about cricket, I know, and only come here to loaf. Mr. — and I are going to drive to Burnham Beeches this afternoon, and walk back after tea. You and Sawnders can come too, and when you see Weston, you may request the pleasure of his company, if his engagements in Sixpenny and his numerous punishments will permit.'

'Oh, thank you, sir; that will be jolly!'

So the little boys scudded off in search of Tommy, whom they found with his head in a basin of water, preparing for dinner. They communicated their tutor's message, while he sputtered in his towel. Tommy was already relatively for his age a celebrity in the cricketing world, and doubted if a whole after-four could be spared from that game.

'As to the pœnas, to-morrow's Sunday, and I shall have lots of time to do them. I've only got the eleven o'clock lesson to write out and translate four times, and a hundred lines, and three copies of extra work. Well, hang Six-penny for once; I'll devote this afternoon to the beauties of nature.'

'I like tea at that cottage,' said Sawnders meditatively. 'They have such good bread and butter, and real cream, and I shouldn't wonder if tutor took a cake.'

'Sawnders, you're a white hog,' said Tommy; 'Skinny and I are above such trifles. I hope there'll be jam.'

It was a lovely afternoon in the late hay-harvest, and the drive was delightful. The last of the wild roses still lingered in the hedges, and the little grass that remained uncut was starred with great white field daisies. The boys on the back seat of the fly, in change coats and straw hats, were in a holiday mood, and full of silly talk. Tommy had mounted the box, and sat beside the driver, of whom he was an old friend, and it was not till the vehicle very nearly carried away the gate-post on Dorney Common that he was discovered to be in possession of the reins.

'We had better leave Eton by the quiet way,' his tutor had said; 'there are so many of the authorities who have just claims on Weston's leisure, that we shall never get him safe out of the place if we attempt to drive through College.'

Of this delightful man's pleasant relations with his pupils I have spoken elsewhere. Mr. Ebbesley, who had been brought up at a private school, and in the good old days when boys regarded their schoolmaster as their natural enemy, had looked forward, not, it is to be feared, with unmixed dissatisfaction, to the idea that his son would turn to him for sympathy and help in the inevitable scrapes which official severity was apt to magnify into crimes. He had made his first visit to Eton after Tim's admission prepared of course to uphold authority and do all that was right and proper, but determined not to be too severe with the boy for his transgressions of the rigid letter of school law; he was going to be very large-minded and understanding. And behold! there had been nothing to sympathise about; above all, nothing to condone. The little boy was so law-abiding that he could have lived without transgression under a far stricter code, and whereas he had been cold and somewhat uncommunicative on several other points, he kindled into something very like enthusiasm when he spoke of his tutor's kindness to him. Mr. Ebbesley told himself that he was very glad it was so, but it seemed to him hard to be the only person without the power of awakening his son's affection.

Is it not significant that this chapter, which is the happiest in my story, should be one of the shortest? This was a day in Tim's life in which birds sang and flowers bloomed for him, and for twelve hours the murmur of the sad undercurrent that flows all through his history had faded from the ear. For my part, I am so glad to think of this afternoon's pleasure that he had, that I cannot refrain from leaving it on record, though it does not advance the action of my drama, a consideration which I am well aware a writer is bound to respect. I have been to Burnham at all seasons of the year, from earliest spring, when there is hardly a wash of green on the noble trees, to latest autumn, when the ground is ankle-deep in glorious colour, and it would be hard to say when there is most beauty there. I have never visited the spot in midwinter, but I am quite sure that if one did the familiar glades would have some appropriate charm for his delight, so regularly does each season lend its own especial gifts to deck that favoured place. At Tim's age, as a rule, a love of nature for her own sake is a rare possession; it is a compensation kept to console older people for the loss of so many other enjoyments that then made the world bright to them. But perhaps it was because his young life was so lacking in the ordinary elements of boyish happiness, that this gift of later age was vouchsafed to our little lad. Certainly the sunlight on the smooth gray trunks, and the peculiar dappled shadows on the sward that only beech-leaves can cast, had a secret to tell him on this blest half-holiday, which would have been Hebrew and Greek to his two playmates. I think it must have been this knowledge of the country as the anodyne for bruised hearts, which made *As You Like It* his favourite play, for Tim read Shakespeare, in Mr. Bowdler's edition with which his father had taken care to provide him. Burnham was Tim's Ardennes, and it would hardly have surprised him to come on the cousins walking in the wood while Touchstone lay hard by among the bracken.

By this time, however, he knew too much to communicate such fancies as these to his companions. The three ran down steep places, jumped off banks into heaps of last year's leaves that still lay piled in some of the hollows, and climbed the trees, on one of which Tommy, who was certainly very unlike Orlando in other respects, inscribed his own initials and those of the party, including his tutor, who is ignorant to this day of the liberty taken with his signature.

Tim ran, climbed, and shouted like the others, and enjoyed himself amazingly. He and Sawnders entrenched themselves in a hollow tree which Tommy was to carry by assault armed with a long stick he had found; but the game had to be abandoned on account of Sawnders's not unnatural objection to being hit really hard, which Tommy treated with the most withering scorn.

'It isn't funny to hurt people,' said the injured defender of the tree, ruefully caressing his wounded member; and this led to a discussion on the nature of true wit, which lasted till their tutor came to call them to tea, and inform them parenthetically that they had made themselves look 'even more disgusting objects than usual.'

Then for the first time Tim noticed with some surprise how tired he felt; indeed for a few moments he was so white that the other master who accompanied them, observing him, thought he was going to faint.

'Oh, it's nothing,' said Tim; 'I suppose I've done more than usual to-day. I didn't feel tired till we stopped.'

Sawnders at once discovered that he was quite used up too, but was promptly snubbed by his tutor.

'That little Ebbesley does not look at all strong,' said the other master, when the two men were for a little out of earshot of their young companions; 'are you not anxious about him?'

'He is certainly delicate,' Tim's tutor answered thoughtfully; 'but I hope he may outgrow it in time,' and on the homeward drive he was very careful of Tim.

So happy had the boy been in the guileless amusements of the afternoon that for the time he actually forgot to think of Carol. But as they neared Eton on their return the recollection of their encounter of the morning and the possibility that he had offended him came back with a sudden pang to his mind — a pang which was proved to be quite superfluous the very next day.

It was Sunday morning, an ideal bright summer Sunday, and Carol was standing at his tutor's door in rather a chastened frame of mind. The bells were ringing for service, and from out the houses the boys were issuing, each in his best clothes and with a generally brushed-up appearance. The sun shone upon the house opposite, and made little silver shields of the leaves of the magnolia that was trained against it. Carol was thinking regretfully how few more Sundays he should sit in the dear familiar chapel, a boy among boys; and looking back across the happy years of his school-life, — hardly a cloud had dimmed their brightness; — in retrospect they seemed one unbroken march of friendliness, gaiety, pleasure, and modest triumph. Eton had treated him very kindly, and he was sorry to leave. Just then who should come out but little Tim. He had recovered to some extent from his fatigue of the day before, and had refused to stay out, though his tutor had suggested the legitimacy of such a course if he were so inclined.

As it chanced, the two were alone. Carol laid a kind hand upon him and called him 'Tim.' The old nickname brought a quick flush of pleasure into the colourless face; at Eton Carol always called him 'Ebbesley.'

'It's a great pity, Tim,' the big boy was saying, 'that we've seen so little of one another; that's the worst of this place, everything goes in layers. If a fellow isn't in your division, with the best will in the world you can never see anything of him.'

'You've always been very good to me, Darley,' Tim answered gratefully.

'You won't have to call me "Darley" any more now I'm leaving. I say, Tim, will you write to me sometimes next half and tell me all about the old place? All my friends of my own standing are leaving too; and after all, you know, you are really the oldest friend of them all.'

'Oh, Carol, may I?' cried Tim; but just then an eruption of other boys occurring from the narrow doorway, he departed to chapel without expressing himself further. He trod upon air; Carol had called him by his old name, and bade, him do the like by him, had spoken of their long friendship, had asked him to write to him. And he had been thinking he had offended him! Tim offered up genuine thanksgivings in the old chapel, where so many generations of boys have knelt on the threshold of life, as he and Carol were kneeling then.

It happened that morning that the first lesson was the beautiful lament of David over his dead friend Jonathan; and Tim, listening to the history of those two friends long ago, felt his love for his friend almost a religion to him. 'Thy love to me was wonderful,' said the voice of the reader, 'passing the love of woman.'

'What woman could ever love him as I do?' thought Tim, as he looked naturally to the seat where Carol sat. At that moment a sunbeam from some hole high in the roof fell on the golden curly head which seemed transfigured; and as Tim's hungry eyes rested on the face of his friend, he turned towards him and smiled upon him in his place.

CHAPTER VIII

Maud is not seventeen,
But she is tall and stately.

Tennyson's *Maud.*

Carol and Tim travelled home together at the end of the half, speeding through the golden summer. It was early August, and everywhere the full-eared grain swayed ripe for the sickle. Here and there the harvest had already begun to be gathered in, and the fields were dotted with the reapers, cutting and binding into sheaves. Larks full-throated hung poised in the quivering air, the woods were in their richest summer green; poppies in field and hedgerow, geraniums on lawn and terrace, blazed each its own scarlet. Shadows were small and black, and lights broad and warm. And above all stretched the sky, cloudless to the horizon, and blue as Carol's eyes.

To be nearly nineteen, to have left school behind one, to be six feet high, to have fine broad shoulders, and a brown, honest, handsome face, good teeth, good spirits, and a good digestion—surely if any one may fairly be called happy in this world, it would be the favoured possessor of all these good things. And yet Carol, who was all this, and more too, was pensive as he sat with his newspaper on his knees and stared out of window. Leaving school is one of the first regrets of a purely sentimental nature, that boys meet with in life, and it lends a tinge of romance to existence. To have come to the end of anything, pleasant or otherwise, is always rather a solemn thing. To fold and lay aside a period of our life, saying, 'Whatever comes or goes, *that* is done with and cannot return,' must have a sobering effect, with however high a courage we turn to meet the untried. People with whom most things go pretty smoothly are apt to think that the happy time just past is the happiest of their lives, and indeed I doubt if at any later date a healthy popular boy is likely to taste such pure joys as during the last few years of his public-school life. It was the first time that Carol had ever been in any but the highest spirits at going home to Darley. Tim, you may be sure, respected his companion's mood, and made but few attempts at conversation; the feeling of class distinction between 'upper division' and 'Remove' was still strong upon him, and kept him rather constrained. He would have been hardly less at ease with the Emperor of Russia, had he encountered that autocrat in a first-class carriage, than with this other boy scarcely older than himself in the eyes of their elders, — for whom the distances between the various stages of boyhood get foreshortened and lost, like the distances between the stars; both are so very far away. But Carol, now he had burst the trammels of Eton conventionalism, meant to see more of Tim, for whom he had always entertained a friendly feeling, and as a first step towards this footing of greater intimacy, invited him to come up and see him next day, when they would go for a walk together. So the next afternoon, when the shadows were beginning almost imperceptibly to lengthen, Tim skipped off, heart elate, for the Court. His way lay through pleasant shady woods, and past the memorable coppice where the accident had occurred, nearly six years before, which had first brought him acquainted with Carol. Much of the old childish Tim lingered in his nature, round the alien growth of the last two years, and he was seized with a sudden longing to revisit the scene of their first meeting. He parted the rods carefully, and stepped into the thicket, finding as nearly as possible the exact spot where he had sat. Let us leave him kneeling there, and go before him to the Court, nor seek to pry into that cool shade of hazel boughs.

In front of the door at Darley Court — not the state entrance with the tall flight of steps and the Doric portico, but the little side-door more generally used — is a stone porch overgrown with clematis and honeysuckle, and containing two benches. On the afternoon in question it was pleasantly screened by its festoons of creepers from the western sun, which blazed hotly on the gravel before it, where two fox-terriers were lying on their sides enjoying the roasting that is distasteful to the lords of the creation. The stillness and hush of a hot day had fallen on the big house, in which nothing seemed alive. The blinds were pulled down, and an artificial twilight reigned in the darkened rooms. Even the gray parrot was too lazy to talk. On one of the benches in the porch, in keeping with the drowsiness around him, Carol was stretched in an attitude of loose-limbed repose, awaiting his small friend. He made no effort to read the book in his hand, but was watching with a listless eye the apparently purposeless gyrations of a pair of white butterflies that were flitting round the honeysuckle blossoms, the only bit of active life in all the still picture. They darted and whirled and turned over and over one another in endless play, only broken now and then by a moment's rest with folded wings on some leaf or tendril. One of the dogs got up and passed round the corner of the house with that slow waddle which dogs adopt between sleeping and sleeping, as though they were afraid of waking themselves too thoroughly in the short interval. By and by the other followed, finding the sun-baked gravel too hot even for him, and Carol was left alone. He was conscious of a delightful sensation of relaxation, such as he remembered to have experienced in a hot bath after a day's hunting; he had abstracted a big cushion from the library sofa as he came out, and rammed it into the small of his back. What wonder that as he watched the sports of the two butterflies he felt his eyes grow heavy, and the narcotic influence of his surroundings beginning to tell upon him, he gradually fell asleep.

For a while the profoundest silence rested on the scene — silence broken at last by the voices of women coming up the carriage-drive.

'I *do* hope they'll be at home, mamma; I must rest after this dreadful walk.'

The speaker was a tall slim girl of about sixteen, dressed in cool white linen.

'My dear child,' says mamma, a no longer blooming, but still pretty woman, who was swaying a pearl-coloured parasol over her broad gray hat and draperies of lavender muslin, 'I have no doubt they will let us sit down for a little, even if Mrs. Darley is not at home.'

'But suppose she *is* at home and says she isn't. Old ladies always go to sleep on hot afternoons, or take off their caps, or something. Then if we ask to go in, what will the poor butler do? That would be a terrible situation. Do you remember when they said "Not at home" at the Chillworthys', and papa insisted on seeing the cedars on the lawn, and there were the whole party having tea? I never shall forget it. I thought my ears would take a week to get white again; and the footman had to say he "found his mistress had come back." She had on thin morocco shoes and a white dressing-gown, which is not the dress one usually puts on for walking.'

'Dearest Violet, it was most awkward; don't refer to it. Perhaps, as you say, we had better not say anything about resting. I noticed a seat as we came up the drive; we can sit down there.'

'And have no tea, and be too late for it at home! Oh, mamma, why do we make calls when the pony's lame? It is almost indecent to go hot and dishevelled into people's drawing-rooms, and with dust on one's boots.'

Violet is going to be a pretty girl; indeed, as she is well aware, she has already considerable personal attractions: soft brown hair, with red lights, a little rippled on her temples; brown eyes full of merriment, shaded by long dark chestnut lashes, and arched by finely pencilled brows; a very fair skin, flushed now with her hot walk, and slightly freckled about the small straight nose; and, rarest of all beauties in a Northern face, a neat pretty mouth and chin. In her white dress and green ribbons, she is very pleasantly noticeable, as she steps firmly along beside her languid mother. It is characteristic that it is she who complains of the heat, though her step is elastic and figure erect, while her mother, every curve of whose rounded form expresses the last stage of graceful lassitude, endeavours to show the bright side of the picture.

'It will be much cooler going home, dear; the sun seems to have less power already; to be sure, we are in shade just here, which may have something to do with it.'

'Oh! mamma dear, of course it has everything to do with it; why, it is barely five, and at this time of year the sun doesn't set till long after seven, and the lower it gets the more it blazes.'

Thus talking they arrived at the porch, which on all but state occasions served as front door at Darley, and Violet, who was a little ahead, stopped short on the threshold, and looked back at her mother with a gleam of fun in her arch eyes.

'Why don't you ring the bell, dear?' asked that lady.

'Come and see,' replied her daughter. The reason is soon apparent. Just below the bell the broad back of a youth was resting against the wall; his arms were crossed and his chin sunk forward on his breast.

'Well. Some one is at home anyway,' whispered the girl, 'and it is not only old ladies who go to sleep on hot afternoons, it seems: this must be "Carol."' (By a fine inflection of voice she expressed, maidenly, that the familiar appellation was meant to be in quotation marks, and was not used by her on her own account.) 'What fun!'

'Hush, oh! hush, dear; if he should wake and hear you!'

'Well? it seems the shortest way out of the difficulty,' retorted Violet.

'How very awkward,' said the poor lady, resorting to a favourite phrase of hers. 'Had we not perhaps better go away, dear?'

But against this Violet protested; she had not walked all this way, to go again without so much as leaving a card; besides (though she only thought this), she had some curiosity to see what the sleeper would look like when awake. 'I shall ring,' she said.

'On no account, Violet! I desire, I insist; so awkward!' cried her mother in an imperative whisper, clutching the hand which the girl was already raising. 'Perhaps I will. Oh dear! anyway better than you,' and she tremblingly extended her own hand across the head of the unconscious Carol. But at this moment one of the terriers, roused by the sound of strange voices, looked round the corner and barked, and Carol's eyes opened with a start, to find a strange lady with outstretched palm, apparently in the act of blessing him. It would be hard to say whether she or Carol blushed the more when, more fully roused to the situation, he had risen and stood before her.

'So awkward,' she began, from force of habit; and then feeling that this was not at all what might be expected of her, she continued, 'Mr. Carol Darley, I suppose — heard of you from Mrs. Darley — going to try and find her at home — only lately come to live in the neighbourhood — must introduce myself — Mrs. Markham Willis; my daughter, Miss Markham Willis'; and Mr. Carol made a fine bow to the young lady, of whose presence he now first became aware.

Mrs. Darley was produced presently from some mysterious seclusion, where she had probably been occupied much as Miss Violet had irreverently supposed. Carol's grandmother was a little pink-and-white old lady, with prim sausage curls of the softest flossy white hair on her forehead. She wore beautiful caps, trimmed with wonderful brocaded ribbon, and a great quantity of minute old-fashioned lockets and brooches.

'I see you have made acquaintance with our boy,' she said. 'Carol dear, tell your Aunt Kate that Mrs. Wallis is here.'

She had never got her husband's name right till they had been married a year, and so, as the Squire used to say when he teased her, could not be expected to remember other people's, but she brought out the mangled words with such a winning graciousness and such an entire belief in herself, that no one thought of being offended, or even surprised. She had called Mr. Ebbesley 'Eversley,' 'Etherington,' and 'Ebbrington' within the first half-hour of their acquaintance, and Tim was either 'Jim or 'Tom,' as it happened.

'How kind of you to come and see me such a hot afternoon,' she went on. 'You must be tired to death. You must have some tea. Kate, dear,' as Carol reappeared with his aunt, 'never mind saying how-d'ye-do. Mrs. Williams will excuse you, I know, while you tell them to get her some tea as soon as possible; it will be better than ceremony this hot weather; and, Kate, some of the little ginger-bread cakes. You are not too old to like cake, dear,' laying a kind old hand on Violet. 'As for Carol, he can't have enough of them; that boy will eat me out of house and home.'

'Yes; you must eat our ginger-bread,' said Carol, laughing. 'Grandmamma has a wonderful recipe that has come down through generations of grandmammas, till it has caught quite a smell of hot ginger-bread.'

The tea was not long in making its appearance; it was good at the Court, like everything else, and was drunk out of little old Worcester cups, which the present occupant keeps in a tall cabinet, but which were then used every day.

Mrs. Markham Willis, who was one of the earliest victims of the now raging china mania, was in ecstasies over the cups, and wanted to know their date and history and all about them; indeed, if her daughter had not stopped her, she would have turned hers upside down to look at the mark, regardless of consequences; as it was, she held it high and tried to peep underneath it.

'My father-in-law gave them to us; they were his mother's,' said Mrs. Darley; 'the year after our marriage it was, 1817. I remember because of Princess Charlotte's death, and we all had to wear mourning; but you are too young to remember, my dear' (she called every one 'my dear'). And as Mrs. Markham Willis had been born some ten years after that sad event, there was no gainsaying the truth of the old lady's statement.

Carol meanwhile was making himself agreeable to Violet, and by the time Tim arrived for the promised walk, they were getting on very comfortably together, considering their uncomfortable ages and still more uncomfortable manner of introduction. So much so, indeed, that Violet was not altogether pleased with the interruption. And any girl might be excused for liking to talk to Carol; he was so big and handsome, so easy and yet so unassuming in manner, that she wished her father could afford to send her brothers to Eton, if this was a specimen of the productions of that school.

They were not a large party, and three out of the five were already known to Tim, but the impression conveyed to him when the door was opened for his entrance, was that of a large company of strangers engaged in animated conversation. Tim's experience of female society was derived principally from that of Mrs. Quitchett, and he was not at home with ladies; he had an uncomfortable feeling that women would despise him for being small for his age and weak, having gathered from his varied reading the idea that they liked in the opposite sex such qualities as were most of a contrast to themselves. Like most people who have seen very few of their fellow-creatures, he was absurdly self-conscious, and the eight feminine eyes turned upon him as he entered the drawing-room exercised a most bewildering effect on him. Carol came to his rescue with quick kindliness, taking him by the hand and introducing him to the two strangers.

'It is *so* pleasant to see so many young people about one.' said Mrs. Markham Willis graciously, which threw poor Tim into yet fresh agitation, as he was painfully aware that he was not at all what was expected in a young person, and feared that if Mrs. Markham Willis really did like young people about her, and thought that she had found one in him, she would be disappointed. It is such a common form of egoism in children, and one not perhaps altogether unknown to older people, thus to exaggerate the importance of their relation to others, who have most likely never thought at all about them.

'Is Mr. Heatherly at home now?' asked Mrs. Darley sweetly.

'"Ebbesley," mamma,' said Miss Kate.

'Well, dear, I said so,' returned her mother, quite unruffled, adding sweetly to Tim, 'We see so little of him here.'

'He is expected to-morrow,' answered the boy, who was occupied in balancing his cup, which would slide ominously about the flat saucer, and trying not to crumb his gingerbread on the carpet. 'He wrote to me that he couldn't get back before; he is a good deal away; I am to meet him at Granthurst.' The cup made a sudden excursion to the very edge of the saucer, and Tim just saved it, turning hot and cold at once at the thought of what might have happened. After this, he refused any more with what was almost a shudder, and Mrs. Markham Willis, who had been pensively regarding the company with her head on one side, remarked, 'I am afraid we really *must* go.' as if it were the outcome of a long conversation, in which all the others had been pressing her to stay. In the confusion of hunting for the pearl-coloured parasol, which she had herself put behind her on sitting down, Carol whispered to Tim, 'You won't mind our walk being a little cut down, old fellow. I must see these people home, but you will come with us, and we can have a little turn after we've left them.' What could Tim say but, 'Oh yes, just as you like'? And so Carol offered his services as an escort, and the four set out together.

'I don't think Mrs. Wilkes a very interesting woman, dear,' said Mrs. Darley to her daughter when the visitors were gone. 'She doesn't seem to me to care much for anything but cups and saucers; she asked me why I didn't put these on the cabinet instead of those pretty vases your father bought last time we were in London; and it is so tiresome of people to have two names. Now I can generally remember one, but two is too much.'

Miss Kate smiled, and turned the conversation to Violet's beauty; on which subject Master Carol also descanted a little later, when, having deposited the young lady and her mamma at their own door, the two lads were going slowly across the fields to the old manor-house. The sun slanting slowly westwards made their shadows long upon the grass as they walked. Bess and Carol's terriers trotted on before them, the former slowly lurching in a slightly sidelong manner, but with infinite dignity as became her years, the two smaller dogs jumping hither and thither, and poking their inquisitive noses into every hole in the hedge.

'Don't you think,' Carol was saying, 'that that Miss Markham Willis is a very pretty girl?'

'Well, really,' answered Tim, 'I daresay she is. Do you know, I don't think I thought much about it; I noticed she had a very nice white dress, but I didn't see much of her face; it was rather dark in the drawing-room, and going home you and she were walking on ahead, so that I only saw her back.'

'Here, Nip; here, Scamp, you little beasts! come out of that!' called Carol, and added pensively, 'Yes, she is pretty; at least I think she *will* be,' with the calm superiority of a man of the world.

'Why, how old do you suppose she is, then?'

'She's sixteen, she told me – quite a child; though when she comes out next year she will treat me as a mere boy, and think herself far above me. Did you see the score Potts made for Kent the other day? Odd he should have made duck at Lords.'

So the conversation drifted off to cricket, in which, as in how many other things, Tim took a profound interest as long as Carol talked of them.

After a time the talk fell on school matters.

Carol, like most boys who have lately left, was full of anecdotes of what had happened 'up to' this master and that; how Smith major once showed up the same pœna, a hundred lines of Virgil, three times to a short-sighted and long-suffering instructor, once for an *Æneid*, once for write out and translate the lesson, and once for a book of *Paradise Lost;* with many other such edifying details, to all of which winged words his steadfast admirer lent a greedy ear. From such stories as these, they passed to more personal reminiscences, and Tim was forced to confess that his early life at Eton had not been altogether a bed of roses.

'I was rather a brute not to see more of you there,' said Carol, 'but then boys *are* brutes.'

Oh, high new standpoint from which to look back and speak of 'boys'!

'Indeed, indeed, I did not think so, Darley – Carol, I mean; you were as good as possible to me; you could not do more; you had all your friends before I came, and you were so much higher up, and –'

'You're a good little soul, Tim,' Carol interrupted, 'and believe in every one; you'd make excuses for a man who robbed and murdered you.'

'But you never robbed and murdered me,' the little boy answered, venturing to be facetious for the first time. 'I am sure you did all you could, and took me for your fag and everything. I'm glad I shall be in Fifth Form next half, for I should never get used to fagging for any one else.'

'Oh, I don't know about that,' said the other deprecatingly, 'but anyway now we are Carol and Tim again, and no longer upper division and lower boy; I hope we may be friends. You will have to write me full accounts of the old place; most of my friends have left, so if you don't I shall never hear anything. Mind you tell me what new boys there are at my tutor's next half, and if any of 'em can play football, and what new choices Harcourt gives their colours to, and who are likely to give us trouble for the cup.'

'How funnily it all came about, Carol,' said Tim modestly, after promising faithfully to comply with all these injunctions, – 'my having you for a friend, I mean. One would have thought I was the last person you would ever have noticed. I can't play football, or anything you like; indeed, I'm no good at any games.'

'You give me a good character,' answered his friend, laughing, 'to suppose me the brutal athlete who selects his friends by their muscle; you don't give me much credit, it seems, for intellectual tastes. Seriously though,' he added, looking down at him kindly, 'you are a first-rate little friend, and will be my link with the dear old place.'

Tim was silent, feeling very grateful and happy.

'I hope nothing will ever break our friendship,' he said presently.

'Oh! nothing ever will,' replied the other airily; 'at least it will be your fault if it does.'

Would it be his fault? Tim smiled at the idea. Would he ever be the one to cast aside what he most valued in all the world? He dwelt upon the thought with some amusement; it seemed too absurd even for protest. Could any one have foretold to us last year eight out of ten of the things that have befallen us in this, how we should have laughed at them! Still, though Tim laughed, one thought seemed to oppress him even in his mirth; it was an odd feeling too indefinite to be called an apprehension, and it had its root and origin in Violet. She was the first young girl he had ever seen placed in juxtaposition to Carol, and the sight of the two together, and his friend's chance remarks upon her beauty, had opened up quite a new vista of possibilities to him. We may laugh at the notion of any one forecasting results from the meeting of a lad of eighteen and a girl of Violet's age, but we must remember the augur himself was but fourteen, and that to him these other two seemed almost more than grown up. He had come to look on Carol as crowned with all fulfilment, a being to whom no future years could add any power or maturity, and Violet was tall and self-possessed enough for twenty; her position as the eldest of a large family had made her old for her age. All the complications of love and romance, never hitherto included in any of Tim's views of the future, started into threatening being for the first time, the more alarming for their vagueness; they seemed to cast quite a new light upon his favourite text, as he repeated it to himself on his knees after his prayers that night, as his habit was, 'Passing the love of woman,' 'The love of woman'; he had never thought of it that way before. He had supposed it meant mother's love, sister's love, all the good things he had never known, poor child; and could only imagine the love of women generally as being gentler and more loving than men. Would Carol ever be what the books called 'in love'? ever marry? and in this remote and awful contingency could they stay close friends, or had he been assured that day for the first time in words of the friendship he most coveted, only to see it melt from his grasp as he claimed it? In vain he asked these questions of his own heart. Of course, he told himself, some day it was sure to happen; he was a fool not to have thought of it before. But what were the words? *'Passing'* yes, *'passing* the love of woman,' — that part at least he could always keep true.

CHAPTER IX

A little sorrow, a little pleasure,
Fate metes us from the dusty measure
That holds the date of all of us:
We are born with travail and strong crying,
And from the birthday to the dying
The likeness of our life is thus.

Swinburne's *Ilicet*.

'You might come up to-morrow afternoon, if you cared,' Carol had said as they parted, 'and then we could go round by the old mill, as I meant to do to-day, and you would see the new cart-road grandfather is making in the wood.'

And who so ready as Tim! Only, he doubted if his father would get back in time for him to get to the Court after he had been to Granthurst to fetch him. Would Carol leave it open? And Carol had said, 'All right, old fellow; I shan't expect you till I see you'; on which understanding they had parted, Tim standing to watch the tall active figure striding away from the open door of the manor-house, calling his dogs after him.

'He's a fine growed lad, that young Darley,' remarked Mrs. Quitchett, who had come out to welcome her nursling; 'do you remember the day, Master Tim dear, when he came with the grapes, the first time ever he come here?'

'Remember? Oh, nurse,' cried Tim (he always called the old lady 'nurse'), 'he's the noblest, finest fellow going, and I love him better than anybody in the world—except you, dear,' he added quickly, putting his arms about her as he saw a quick look of pain cross her face; and then, what was it? a prick of conscience perhaps that made him add lower and more thoughtfully, with just a shade of doubt in his tone, 'and father.'

Was it true that he loved his father better than Carol? The question had never before suggested itself to him in that crude form. What was the criterion of loving? He did not know; he had no signs to go by. He had assumed, as children do, that of course he loved his father; good people always love their parents. It was only that vague indefinite class of 'the wicked,' which he heard denounced on Sunday, and to which it never occurs to a child that he or any of his immediate surroundings can possibly belong, who did not love their parents. But now he felt in his inmost being that his affection for his father was *not* as strong as that for his friend, — was not, indeed, of the same sort at all, and he took shame to himself for the discovery. Many of us live thus for years, allowing our hearts to act for us, and never asking ourselves needless psychological questions; and then suddenly comes a time when we seem to start up uncomfortably active and alert, new possibilities open out around us, and questionings of our feelings suggest themselves which plead, importunate, for answers. Nor can we make a greater mistake than in supposing that such turns in their lives come only to men and women. To a boy of Tim's organisation, fourteen is an age quite ripe for crises.

Violet crosses his path, erect, slim, and hazel-eyed, and in a moment he seems to understand all possible complications of love and courtship between her and Carol. He makes a chance little gush to his old nurse, and lo! conscience awaking, proceeds to inquire with uncomfortable pertinacity into his relations with his father. When one considers how those who have delicate consciences like our hero, suffer and writhe, and run round and round, and drive their stings into their own brains, one is tempted to ask as the best gift for one's dearest, a fine tough insensibility, a happy bluntness of the moral sense. I suppose the moralists would tell us to keep our account with the stern goddess as clean as possible, to put into her hands no weapon for our torment; but which of us can truly boast of such a course as that? And besides, does not experience daily teach us that it is precisely the most blameless among us she selects for her favourite victims?

Tim, as he sat over the book he did not read that night, as he drove over to Granthurst in the trap next day, could not help asking himself, 'What have I ever done for father, who has done so much for me? What have I ever given up for him? He tried to answer that no boys of his age can do anything for their parents; it is a matter of course that they accept what they get. 'Ah! but,' says conscience, '*they* love their fathers.' And though he dared not put it into words even to himself, the thought was ever present, though formless as yet within him, that he did *not* love his father.

Poor Mr. Ebbesley! no one *did* love him that I know of; no one ever had. He was not made to attract love, and yet if his heart was not breaking for it (not being of a breaking sort), it had hardened and withered and dried up for want of it.

To have longed for love all one's life, to have sought it with care and constantly missed it, is as sad a fate as can well be imposed on a man, and is not calculated to sweeten the temper.

Looking back over William Ebbesley's life, the wonder is that he had not turned out a social pariah and enemy of his race. There must have been an immense moral rectitude about him that kept him true to what he believed to be his duty to his neighbour.

Early left an orphan by poor and improvident parents, he had been educated by the grudging charity of people with a family to provide for, and sent abroad at an age when many boys have not left school, to push his own fortunes. Uncheered, uncared-for, he had fought his way through twenty hard years, if not to riches, to what thirty years ago was considered a very decent competence, and had returned to England to fall a prey to one of those absorbing passions for a beautiful and penniless girl many years younger than himself, which are so often the fate of men verging on middle age, in whose earlier youth there has been no room for romance. On her he had lavished all the wealth of love that had for years accumulated in his lonely heart. I would dwell as lightly as possible on the painful and bitter episode of his short married life; of the way it ended I have already given a hint in an earlier chapter of this story. Just where he had placed all his hopes of happiness, the bitterest shame and sorrow of his life had lain in wait for him.

Many men would have been utterly crushed by such an end of all that they had longed and worked for, and laid down their arms in the unequal struggle with fate. But Ebbesley, half ruined by the extravagance of the woman he had loved, wounded to the heart by her cruelty, and humiliated in every fibre of his proud nature by her unfaithfulness, had yet one link that bound him to the world, one thing left to work for. It was such a fragile thread, the poor little year-old baby, by which to hang on to affection and grace and the beauty of life, but it was his all, and he grasped it despairingly. For the baby's sake he had gone uncomplainingly back to years more of the banishment he had thought ended, and the labour he believed accomplished, even separating himself from the child for the child's good. We have seen how he dwelt in secret on what his son was to look like, and be like; how often in his own mind he had foreseen the manner of their meeting; and how, when the time was come, he had chafed at every delay, counting trains and steamboats but crawling snails compared to the wings of love that were bearing him back to his little one. And we have seen too what awaited him at home. If I have wearied my reader with insisting on the barrenness of this man's life, it is because I am full of pity for him, and would not have him judged too hardly, if in what follows he seems unkind to his son.

Tim arrived at Granthurst in a chastened frame of mind, and endeavoured to blot himself out of the gaze of the few unemployed people always waiting about a station, who seized on him as lawful prey, and stared as though with a view to his identification on the morrow before a jury of their fellow-citizens. From this scrutiny, which was peculiarly trying and distasteful to him, he was shortly delivered by the arrival of a hot dog, who was brought in resisting violently and tied to a post, and upon whom all the interest of the unoccupied population, for a moment directed at him, fastened itself with avidity, leaving Tim once more to his compunctions. The first outcome of his meditations was an unusual infusion of tenderness and spontaneity in the greeting kiss he bestowed upon his father, when in due course the train brought up beside the platform, and Mr. Ebbesley descended, bending a cindery whisker towards the fresh young lips.

As they were mounting into their conveyance, and the aggressive whiteness of the 'W. E.,' which from the side of his black bag thrust its owner's personality on a reluctant public, was being eclipsed under the seat, a new anxiety suggested itself to Tim, which his previous train of thought had for the time kept under. Mindful of Carol's invitation, he consulted his watch, and found that his power to avail himself of it would depend upon whether Mr. Ebbesley had any business in Granthurst, or meant to return at once to Stoke Ashton; timidly, but with a manner of studied unconcern, he asked the question, and to his delight his father answered that he was going straight home. It seemed as though his mind in its rebound, as this weight was lifted off it, scattered the doubts and fears that had oppressed it all the morning, and he felt light of heart, and inclined to chatter as the carriage rolled on its way over breezy commons, or plunged into deep shady lanes. In the days when Tim was a schoolboy August was still a hot month, and the warm sun called an unusual glow into his cheek at the edge of the shadow cast by his straw hat with its pretty ribbon.

'Eton has certainly improved him,' thought Mr. Ebbesley, looking at him half critically; 'he has lost his whipped-dog expression,' and he smiled approvingly at his son, saying with frosty geniality, 'You must tell me all about last half; how have you been doing at school?'

'Oh! it has been a very jolly half, and I have hardly stayed out at all, although it was so hot. I wrote you that I took 13th in trials. Tommy Weston said it was an unlucky number, but I told him he would not have thought so if he had been there in the list instead of 25th.'

'And who is Tommy Weston?' asked Mr. Ebbesley, feeling quite friendly towards this other man's son who had done less well than his own.

'Tommy isn't his real name, you know,' explained Tim; 'he's a fellow at m'-tutor's, and the other fellows call him Tommy; he's been very jolly to me, and, indeed, I get on better with all the fellows than I did at first. And I've "passed," which means, don't you know, that I can swim, and may go on the river, and I *think*,' rather doubtfully, 'I'm beginning to like cricket a little.'

'That's a good thing,' said his father judicially; 'it is always well in life to like what other people like; eccentricity always brings unhappiness.'

Tim glowed and expanded with the pleasant sense of having done the right thing; it was such a new and strange sensation. 'And I've grown,' he said exultingly; 'I'm two inches taller than I was in the spring.'

'Capital,' said Mr. Ebbesley, almost with enthusiasm; and he thought, 'It is not always the boys who grow young who turn out the finest men in the end.' 'And your tutor?' he asked; 'I hope he is satisfied with you.'

'Oh! m'-tutor's been awfully good to me; he always is; he took me to Burnham Beeches the other day, and we had a delightful afternoon, and he's promised to give me a good report. I was 5th in collections, and if I had been 3d I should have got a prize; so tutor said he would give me a little book anyway, and he wrote "to console" in it, because he said it was hard luck on me being just out of it, and I had worked very well all the half. Wasn't it kind of him?'

In his heart Mr. Ebbesley thought it was a foolish indulgence, but he was feeling so amiably towards his son just then that he let it pass without comment. Indeed, he seemed altogether in so gracious a mood as he sat listening with a grave smile to all that he was told, though he did not say much, that Tim was presently encouraged, rambling from one subject to another, to speak of Carol. He had never felt so near to his father before, so able to talk freely to him of what was in his heart. Ordinarily he did not say much about his friend; his father never seemed to be pleased at his affection for him. To tell the truth, the poor man had not forgiven Carol the awkwardness of their first meeting, and the innocent part he had borne in the disappointment of all his most cherished expectations. And it was not enough that this boy who was not his, by keeping before his eyes the perfect realisation of all that he had desired in his own son, seemed always to mock him; but he must needs come between him and that son, such as he was, and steal the affections that were his by every right, and add to the wealth of love lavished on him by his own kinsfolk. Truly, 'to him that hath shall be given, and from him that hath not shall be taken away even that which he hath.' It was by a law as natural as that of gravitation that the ewe-lamb was added to the flocks and herds of the rich man, and the wonder is that Nathan should have seen anything odd in the arrangement. Still this is a hard saying, and a view of matters that has seemed unjust to generations of men, from the prophet down to

William Ebbesley, who certainly needed and would have appreciated a little affection far more than the fortunate Carol. In fact, he was jealous; and strange as it may seem that a father should be jealous of his son's friends, it is by no means so rare a thing as might be supposed. No parent can help a certain humiliation and annoyance at the thought of a child's undoubted preference of another to himself. Many people under these circumstances make the grievous mistake of trying to separate their sons from the objects of their jealousy, but in no case is this treatment successful. Some lads turn sulky under it, and nurse bitter feelings in secret, while others break out into open defiance and rebellion, when all sorts of trouble ensue. Of course the parents do not admit for a moment that it is jealousy that prompts their course; there are always admirable reasons why the objectionable person is not a good friend for their offspring. Mr. Ebbesley would probably have repudiated with scorn the idea of his being jealous of Tim's affection for Carol Darley, but it galled and irritated him none the less; until he had come to entertain such a hearty dislike of his young neighbour as he would have been slow to acknowledge even to himself. He did not consider how little pains he had taken to secure the gift which he grudged to another; in his own way he loved his son strongly, but not having found him such as he had hoped, he could not give him that approving affection which alone conveys the *idea* of love to a child's mind. All the same, it did not strike him as anything less than reasonable to expect that the boy should be intuitively aware of this hidden love of his, and respond to it as warmly as though it were expressed. He knew he had the feeling, but did not reflect that he never showed it. And though Tim was as far from guessing his father's real sentiments with regard to his friend as he was from divining his love for himself, he felt instinctively, though dimly, that the subject of Carol was not a welcome one to Mr. Ebbesley, and that he would therefore do well, without actually disguising the fact of his intimacy with him, to see him quietly, and talk of him as little as possible. And this was not a difficult course to pursue, as Mr. Ebbesley rarely encouraged much conversation from him on any subject, and still more rarely made any inquiries as to where, how, or with whom he spent his time when they were apart.

But on this particular afternoon he seemed, as I have said, so kind, and Tim was feeling so warmly towards him, and everything was working so well towards the gratification of his wish to be off to the Court in time for the promised walk, that he said in the lightness of his heart, 'I am glad you had no business in Granthurst, father.'

'Why so?' asked his father, wondering in his own mind if he were going to suggest their doing anything together, and determined beforehand to accede to any such proposition, even though he had to put off looking over the law-papers he had brought down with him till the next day.

'Well, you see, I was to have gone a walk with Carol Darley yesterday, but there were people calling at the Court, and he had to go back with them, so we couldn't have our walk. And he said we might go this afternoon, but I wasn't sure if I should be back in time; if you'd had to stay in Granthurst it would have made it too late. So we left it open. It was to depend on that. That's why I wanted to know if you were coming straight home. I'm awfully glad.'

It was one of Mr. Ebbesley's idiosyncrasies that he always paused before answering any one just long enough to make his interlocutor feel awkwardly uncertain whether he had heard or not; so that Tim, who was accustomed to his ways, was not for a moment or two surprised at his silence.

When he did speak it was to say slowly, and in a voice from which all traces either of affection or resentment were equally removed —

'You say you were at Darley Court yesterday; am I to understand that you wish to go there again to-day?'

Tim looked up quickly, and was startled at the hard expression on his father's face.

'Yes.' he stammered; 'I thought, I meant — '

'I think you will be in the way,' Mr. Ebbesley continued, in the same measured tones. 'Mr. and Mrs. Darley cannot want you perpetually about the house.'

'But most likely I should not see any of them,' Tim protested eagerly. 'I am only going to see Carol; it was quite by accident that he happened to be in the drawing-room yesterday when I went.'

'I should think he too could exist without seeing you *every* day,' said his father sharply, and then relapsing into stateliness, he added, ' I disapprove of such violent intimacies, especially with people with whom I am not intimate myself.'

It flashed across Tim that if his intimacies were to be regulated by his father's, their number would indeed be limited. But he swallowed this repartee and made one despairing effort. 'But he *asked* me to come, and I said I would. I will not go again if you don't like me to — '

'I desire,' said Mr. Ebbesley, in a way that put an end to all further discussion of the subject, 'that you will not go to the Court this afternoon. That is enough.'

No word of *why* he wanted him to stay at the manor-house, of regret that he should wish to leave him on the first afternoon that they were together after so long a separation; he was too proud to show his own child how much he needed his affection. Nothing could be farther from Tim's imagination than that his father should wish to keep him near himself, or have any desire for his company. Probably one indication of a human motive, even a jealous or selfish one, that had its root in love, would have brought them closer together than anything had ever done yet, but it was foreign to William Ebbesley's nature to make such a sign; he believed himself to be actuated by entirely impersonal considerations, or at least he wished to believe so, and was determined that his son should, whether he did or not. So Tim's flutterings of love and joy born of a summer's morning were chilled back upon his heart, and he sat in silence for the rest of the drive sore and resentful, and escaped as soon as they reached home to cry in his own room alone with Bess. Carol, concluding that he had not got back in time, visited the old mill and the new cart-road by himself, whistling as he went.

This was Mr. Ebbesley's first act of open hostility to the friendship between the lads, and it was the beginning of much pain and heart-burning to Tim, serving to widen the distance between him and his father considerably.

CHAPTER X

Oh let the solid ground
Not fail beneath my feet
Before my life has found
What some have found so sweet.

Tennyson's *Maud.*

Tim's career at Eton, after it became more prosperous, offers nothing of much interest to the general public, his relations with the various good people who befriended him having nothing to do with this story, which is the history of his friendship for Carol, and for no one else. We must not suppose, however, that he had no other friends. He was not of the very successful type, but he made several very fast and true ones at this period of his life. His tutor was very fond of him, and more than one boy among his schoolfellows asked him to visit him in the holidays, which is the highest mark of esteem that young gentlemen at that age can confer. His father would have liked him to go, but Tim would accept none of these invitations, feeling how unlike the homes his friends described to him — abodes of mothers and sisters and ponies, and such good things — were to the lonely old manor-house, and not caring to invite their inspection of his own interior in return. Still he felt the kindness of the intention, and was as placidly contented as he could be in a place where Carol had been, and was not; for in spite of new ties and interests, above and below all other friendships or affections, his life-devotion held its undiminished sway. He corresponded regularly with Carol, according to his promise, telling him all the gossip of the old place, so interesting to those who have grown up in that queer nursery, so inscrutably dull to all besides. Many a detail of cricket or fives news was mastered by the indefatigable Tim, though he took but a slender concern in such matters on his own account, because he knew they would be of interest to Carol, who on his side declared our hero the best of correspondents, and supplied him in return with descriptions of Cambridge, or, if at Darley, with constant bulletins of the health of Bess.

'Bess is renewing her youth.' he would write; 'there is not a rabbit but goes in fear for his life in all Stoke Ashton parish. Mrs. Quitchett seems to have borrowed the other old lady's receipt, not for rabbit-hunting, but for looking young. In your absence, she hails me with pleasure, as some one to whom to talk of you.'

Or from Cambridge: 'Do you want to know what I am about? I walk a great deal—to stretch my legs, which you may think do not require it—not to see the country, which a fellow here, who never said anything else good that I know of, said one could do by putting on a pair of high-heeled boots. I read a fairish amount, and play lots of tennis. Do you know what a bisque is? or that half thirty is not the same as fifteen? In the evenings I have taken violently to whist, and have once or twice ventured on more exciting games, but don't feel inclined to become a professional gambler yet awhile. Next winter I think I shall keep a horse. It isn't half a bad life, and there are lots of awfully jolly fellows; but I miss the old school more than I can say, and am still more than half inclined to blub when I think of it. What shall I do next half without Upper Club? I don't believe playing for the University will at all console me.'

Not very deep perhaps, but frank, boyish, jolly letters, with a sensation as of fresh air blowing through them. I have a pile of them from which I could quote, all much in the same style. Years afterwards they were found, oh! how carefully preserved, and tied together in little bundles, with now only the date of their receipt, now some tender comment carefully affixed in Tim's youthful scrawl.

The neatness of their arrangement had something specially touching about it, tidiness not being as a general rule by any means a distinguishing characteristic of their recipient.

As may readily be imagined, Tim's persistence in his intimacy with Carol did not tend to increase the comfort of his relations with his father. Mr. Ebbesley was not a man of many words; but neither was it difficult to see of what he disapproved, and in the present case, without parading his sentiments, he took no pains to conceal them. During the autumn and winter that followed the conversation recorded in the last chapter he confined himself to little sneers and sarcasms when Carol's name happened to be mentioned in his presence, which Tim took care should be as seldom as possible. But the very carefulness of this avoidance was in itself a cause of constraint. How could the boy be at ease with his father when all his most sacred feelings clustered round an object of which he felt it better never to speak to him? To live in tacit defiance of an unexpressed desire of one's nearest relative does not conduce to a comfortable state of things.

It was in the first Easter holidays after the August day when Fate, in the shape of Miss Markham Willis, had first crossed the path of the two friends, that, Carol having gone back to Cambridge before Tim's return to Eton, the latter was one day diligently scribbling his budget of home news in the old manor library where he had lain asleep the day his father's letter had come to Mrs. Quitchett. (What the news was I am not in a position to tell you, because, you see, though I can refer to every line Carol wrote to Tim, I have not the same advantage as regards Tim's answers.) So immersed was he in his writing, and in the mental effort of omitting nothing Carol would like to be told, that he did not hear the door open, nor observe that any one had come in, till he was startled by a shadow falling on the paper, and looking up, was somewhat alarmed to find his father standing before him with an expression which was anything rather than amiable. Mr. Ebbesley had been vexed about something, and was in a mood for finding fault.

'Always scribbling,' he began; 'it's really a sin not to be out this lovely day.'

He was not as a rule keenly susceptible to the beauty of the weather, and his remark therefore rather surprised his son.

'I was out all the morning,' he said.

'Where?' asked his father.

'Oh! up above Beech Farm, in the Court woods,' and Tim blushed a little as he spoke. The fact was he had been making one of his pilgrimages to the sacred spot where his dinner with the squirrel had been interrupted so many years before.

'In the Court woods,' repeated Mr. Ebbesley crossly; 'really I'm ashamed of you. Not content with dangling eternally about after that turnip-eating young embryo squire the whole time he's here, you must needs make yourself ridiculous by hanging about his house and grounds like a sentimental girl when he's away.'

'You shan't call Carol names,' Tim answered hotly, the faint blood in his cheeks suddenly crimsoning them all over; 'he's the best and — There, I beg your pardon; I know I oughtn't to speak so to you, but I couldn't help it. Say what you like about me, but please don't sneer at him.'

'I am sure he would be delighted if he knew what a champion he had in you; don't you see that the fellow doesn't want you? You *must* bore him.'

'You've no right to say he doesn't want me.' the boy flashed out again; 'it's not true; and — and — I think he's the best judge of whether he wants me or not.'

He was quivering all over, but his father took no more notice of this outbreak than of the former one.

'I've no doubt,' he went on, motioning slightly towards the unfinished letter, 'that it's to him you've been writing all this trash. It seems to me that you waste a good deal of your time and my paper in supplying pipe-lighters for unknown undergraduates.'

'What is it you want me to do?' asked Tim hopelessly.

'You know quite well what my wishes are: that I disapprove of violent intimacies and long letter-writing. Why can't you be friends with this very commonplace young man as other people are friends, without all this foolish fuss? I don't want you to waste all your time in writing sentimental letters; it is enervating; and Heaven knows you don't require *that!*'

Tim stood white and uncertain, biting his pen. 'You want me to give Carol up,' he said.

'That is so like you,' said Mr. Ebbesley; 'you make such a tragedy of everything; who talks of giving up? I only ask you for once to show a little common sense, and not eternally to go on being a baby. Why can you never be like other boys about anything, I wonder?'

Tim wondered that too; he also wondered whether it would be worth while to try and make his father understand that his letters were not 'sentimental,' as he called them. For a minute he half felt inclined to ask him to read the one on the table between them, but he recollected all sorts of little simple sayings and phrases that he would not for the world submit to the sarcastic perusal of his father's double eyeglass. *He* knew perfectly well that to continue on terms of cool acquaintance with Carol, always guarding every word and action for fear it was too intimate, and not writing to him after promising to do so, was simply impossible; but he knew too that it was hopeless to make his father see this as he saw it. No. What he meant him to do was simply to give up his friend, and he felt a dull feeling of anger and defiance at what he considered his disingenuous way of putting himself more or less in the right by all this talk about 'common sense' and 'ordinary friendship,' He determined to call things by their right names, and since his father did not like his speaking of what he required of him as 'giving up Carol,' he would do it again.

'I am sorry I cannot obey you,' he said slowly; 'I think one should never give up a friend unless for his own good.'

'Oh! in that case you think you should?' inquired his father, with an ironical appearance of interest.

'Yes; if one loved a person truly, one would do anything for him; even give him up,' answered Tim quite simply.

Mr. Ebbesley fairly lost patience. 'Don't you know I could *make* you do this if I chose?' he said almost fiercely; perhaps the words 'if one loved a person truly' had galled his wound a little. But he relapsed into his manner of carefully assumed indifference to add, 'I prefer, however, to leave you free to find out that I am right by experience; I have warned you, and you will not be warned; you know my wishes, but since you refuse to be guided by them you shall please yourself.' And he turned and left the room.

Tim stood with the unfinished letter in his hand staring blankly after him. Why was the only thing his father had ever asked of him the only thing he could not do? He sank back into his chair and covered his face with the letter. 'Oh! Carol,' he moaned, 'will you cast me off some day after this?'

It would be hard to say whether father or son suffered more keenly after this interview. Tim, to be sure, had carried his point, but his laurels were dear bought, and some victories, as we know, are almost more disastrous than defeats; and then Mr. Ebbesley had the pleasant certainty that he was right, which was his consolation in many of the hard knocks of life. He sincerely believed himself actuated by none but the very highest motives, and, moreover, considered that he had displayed remarkable temper and moderation under very trying circumstances. None the less he had been defied and bested, refused what he had almost stooped to ask, and had flat disobedience and revolt opposed to his expressed wishes. He had imprudently risked a trial of strength with Carol, and been thrown. Not only had he less hold on his son's affections, but actually less power over his actions than this youth who cared, he was convinced, so little for either one or the other. He felt sore and injured, and Tim supremely miserable, for some time; days during which they met and lived together as usual, and tried with very poor success to behave as though nothing had happened. Tim continued to write to Carol, but he did so henceforth in his room, and carried his letters to the post himself, not from a desire to conceal the fact from his father, but only to avoid a recurrence of the painful scene in the library; and indeed it had no successors.

Mr. Ebbesley had delivered himself of his views, and thereafter the grave was not more silent; the subject of Carol was no more mentioned between him and his son. And Tim wrote no word of what had happened to Carol. In the first place, he would have died a thousand deaths sooner than say a word that could distress him, and in the second, he was far too proud to let even his best friend into the secret of his disagreement with his father. His letters flowed on in their usual channel, and if they were a little lacking in spirit, their recipient was by no means an observant critic, and least of all just then, being, as we shall see, much preoccupied with affairs of his own.

For, if Tim's letters were unchanged, Carol's certainly were not. There crept into them about this time a quite new and strange tone, which did not pass unnoticed by his young correspondent. It would be difficult to describe exactly what it was; but chance remarks scattered up and down, together with a certain abstract and speculative turn of sentence quite foreign to the young man's usual style, would have indicated pretty clearly to any one but a baby what was the matter with the writer. 'I feel,' he wrote, 'that I am approaching a turning-point in my life, which will make me either very happy or very miserable; and I feel too that it is for life.' And elsewhere he congratulated Tim on being 'still of an age when he was not likely to know what it was to care more for one person than for all the rest of the world,' at which his friend smiled a little sadly, thinking that he did. There are no notes on these letters in Tim's handwriting, only the date; probably they puzzled the boy not a little.

That Carol was not quite himself seemed pretty clear; then it dawned upon him that his state of mind indicated strong affection for some one, and almost simultaneously he arrived at the chilling conviction that that some one was certainly not himself. He hardly knew how to reply to these strange unfamiliar letters; no doubt he thought he was expected to make some sign of sympathy or interest, but with the vague and fragmentary knowledge he possessed, he felt it impossible to do so. In one way he was undoubtedly the gainer by this mystery. At no previous time had Carol ever written, not only so regularly, but so often; hardly a week passed without his hearing from him, and usually at some length. Still he felt uneasily that something was wrong; and when at the end of the Cambridge May term his friend wrote that he was coming down to Eton for a day or two, he was glad not only with the joy of meeting again, but almost more so at the opportunity thus afforded to him of judging if his voice, look, or manner were in keeping with the strangeness of his epistolary style. And yet he half feared to see in him the probable confirmation of his suspicions of something being wrong.

When Carol did come, his behaviour was even stranger than his writing. Instead of launching himself out on to the pavement over the closed door of his fly the moment it drew up in front of tutor's, and sending a flying glance up the house-front for any friends who might be on the look-out, as was his usual custom, followed by a tremendous shout if his eye caught a familiar face, Tim, who was watching from his window, was amazed to see him sit meekly while the driver descended from his box and opened the door, and then inquire what he owed him, as though he had just taken the drive from Slough Station to Eton for the first time in his life. And having paid the man, who had driven him any time these seven years, and was too much astonished even to overcharge him, he walked into the house without once looking up. Tim sat down and stared. What did it all mean? Nor had he less cause to wonder when Carol came up to visit him; he greeted him with more than ordinary cordiality, and then laughed a little, and then seemed to forget his existence, becoming absorbed in a minute inspection of everything in the room, as if he had never seen it before.

'Holker isn't going to play in the next match,' began Tim, producing the cricket shop he had been carefully storing himself with for Carol's arrival. 'He missed three catches on Tuesday, and as all his chance was for his fielding, Jones has told Tuttiett he'll try him. They say Holker's furious, and swears if he don't get his eleven, it'll be because Jones hates him, and will be sure to spite him if he can.'

'Who's Jones?' inquired Carol dreamily.

Now Jones had been in his own eleven, and they had played together in all the matches only one short year before, not to mention that they had been, as Tim knew, in close correspondence ever since, the ex-captain giving his successor the benefit of his greater experience in all matters relating to the government of the cricket world.

'Who's Jones!' echoed Tim in such unfeigned surprise that Carol pulled himself together, laughed again, and said he wasn't thinking.

They talked about the eleven for a little, but it was obvious that the old boy's heart was not as heretofore in the talk, and presently he wandered to the window, and began pitilessly pulling to pieces one of Tim's best fancy geraniums. Tim's flower-box was his especial pride and glory; he loved and tended his flowers as no other boy in the house did, and it is on record that on one occasion, when he was watering them, and some of the water had gone on the head of the big boy in the room below, who happened to be talking out of the window to a friend, that hero, having come up breathing vengeance, had been so struck with the beauty of the little garden that he had sat down to talk about it, the wooden spoon he had brought with him lying idly in his lap. Ordinarily, Carol would not for the world have injured one of these treasures, as much from dislike of giving pain as from his own feeling towards them, the result of Miss Kate's early training. Tim could stand it no longer.

'Carol,' he said, laying a timid hand on the strong arm that was working havoc among his pelargoniums,' please forgive me for being curious, but isn't there something up? You don't seem like yourself; and your letters have been so rum lately. Is anything wrong? Can I do anything? Won't you tell me what's the matter?'

Carol turned and looked at him; then he took his hand and said gently —

'By Jove, Tim, what a clever little soul you are! fancy your noticing like that. Shall I tell you? After all, I'd sooner tell you than any one; you've always been the best and truest friend a fellow ever had, though there's so much difference in our ages.'

Tim was gratified. 'You've always been so good to me, Carol,' he said, 'and I don't care much for many people.'

'Can you keep a secret?' asked his friend; 'for it *is* a secret at present.'

The tortures of the Inquisition, Tim protested, should not draw a word from him, when Carol had bid him be silent; and then out it all came.

'Why shouldn't he tell him? He might think it odd of him to do so, but tell some one he must, and the fact was, to cut a long story short, he was in love. He remembered Miss Markham Willis—Violet?' (Yes, Tim remembered her, and with her a whole train of old apprehensions.) 'Well, she was the girl he was in love with, and she was the loveliest girl in all England, and the kindest to her little brothers and sisters, and, in fact, the most peerless in all the relations of life; and he knew every one would say they were too young, but he knew what love was, and he saw now that he had loved her ever since they first met, and he should never feel the same for any one else, and Tim wasn't to say a word about it.'

Standing there opposite to him, holding his hands, his honest blue eyes wet with emotion, and his voice that Tim had heard always firm, and sometimes loud, trembling as he made the confession of his young love, there was something beautiful and touching in the great strong boy; he seemed to have lost all his masterfulness, and to be quite meek and uncertain of himself for the first time in his life. And Tim, part frightened, and part regretful, and part gratified at having been selected as confidant on so important an occasion, promised silence,—would have promised anything, in fact, that Carol had demanded,—and Carol, the floodgates of his silence being burst at last, and the tide of his feelings finding free vent, went on and said much more.

Violet and her mother had been staying at Cambridge for the May week with some Head of a college who was their kinsman, and Carol had been bound, in common politeness, to do the honours of his University to his country neighbours; so that was how matters had come to a crisis with him, and the conviction had been borne in upon him in the intervals of boat-races, flower-shows, and dancing that for him there was and would always be but one woman in the world.

'And does she—does she—?' inquired Tim discreetly.

'Ah! there's where it is,' cried the other; 'I think, I really think she likes me, but I didn't dare speak; it seemed as if it couldn't be possible such a girl should really care for me.'

'Not care for *you*!' exclaimed Tim almost angrily, and then he stopped, much embarrassed.

'Oh, you are such a staunch little friend!' said Carol; 'you think much too well of me, don't you know.'

But for all that he was cheered by his friend's enthusiasm; and the mere fact of having unburthened himself to patient and sympathetic ears sent him off more nearly restored to his normal frame of mind, to discuss the new choices with Jones, quite like a sane mortal.

So Carol and Violet fell in love; for it was not many weeks after this that he found the courage he had lacked at Cambridge, and his modest 'thinking she liked him' was converted into triumphant certainty. They were absurdly young of course. Violet was only seventeen and Carol not yet twenty when they first discovered they were made for one another, and mutually imparted this intelligence, as, I am told, is the manner of young people. Of course, too, the old people, as is *their* manner, scouted the notion, and said, 'Nonsense; boy and girl; too young to think of such things.' But the tendency of boys and girls being to get their way in matters of this sort, in spite of much more severe elders than Mr. and Mrs. Markham Willis, or the dear old Darleys, a compromise was at last effected. In two years, when Carol left the University, if he and Violet were still of the same mind the thing should be; but in the meanwhile they were not to be considered engaged, and not to correspond, — a very wise decision, as it seems to me, and one that reflected credit on all concerned. So these two were to wait, as so many others have done, and as they could well afford to do at their age, having life before them, and youth, and good looks, and high spirits to cheer them through their waiting.

Tim was installed as prime confidant, and to him Carol told or wrote all his hopes and fears. When the compromise was extracted from the old people, he came radiant to the manor-house, and finding Tim alone in the garden, poured out all his golden dream to him.

'Two years were quite a short time to wait; many people had to wait half their lives. He would serve for Violet as long as Jacob had for Rachel, if need were; and wasn't it grand of her to promise to wait for him? though of course he could not accept such a promise, and had quite refused to bind her.'

Tim listened to it all, now and then squeezing his friend's hand in token of sympathy and attention; luckily he was not expected to say much, for he would have been rather at a loss what to say. His mind was travelling one year back to the day when he had gone up to the Court and found Violet installed in the drawing-room there; all the thoughts so vague and unintelligible to him then had taken form and substance; now he understood what the shadow was that had fallen across his path that day; that thing he had dimly guessed at had come upon him, and it was to him that Carol looked for rejoicing in his joy. Of course he *did* rejoice, and felt delighted that this new experience of his idol seemed only to bring them nearer together instead of separating them; but was it really so? It is true, he saw more of him than he had ever done before, and when he went away again, heard from him oftener; but the talks and the letters were full of Violet, and of Violet only; she was the cause of it all. If Carol desired his society, it was that to him better than any one he could discourse of her perfections; if he wrote nearly every day, it was that he was not allowed to write to her, and the next best thing was writing about her. Tim was useful only as the safety-valve which allowed him to let off some of the enthusiasm with which he was overflowing. He would have liked to cry the name of his beloved to all the winds; failing that, it was a comfort to hold forth on the subject either with tongue or pen. And Tim saw all this quite plainly, and somehow was not as grateful at being selected for the part he was playing as he felt he should be. 'Would he like it after all,' he asked himself, 'since this thing was to be' (and he bowed before the inevitable), 'had Carol selected any one else to whom to lay open his heart?' He took himself to task for not feeling happier in his friend's happiness. This was not the devotion he had vowed to him in his own heart, this selfishness that put himself before the object of his affection, which refused to dance at the dear one's piping. Somehow he felt it would be easier to lament at his mourning; and for this too he had by and by the opportunity, as we shall see.

CHAPTER XI

Love is strong as death.
Jealousy is cruel as the grave.

Solomons Song.

'He wants great care and attention; there is no use denying it. He is not the sort of lad with whom you can afford to run risks. He has no stamina, none; no constitution. I don't say he is ill. God grant he may not be, for he hasn't the strength to throw things off as some boys do.'

The speaker was the old Stoke Ashton doctor, and the subject of his remarks was Tim. It was a hard winter, and the boy was not very well. He did not outgrow his childish delicacy, though it would be hard to say quite what was the matter with him. Mrs. Quitchett used to trot off to her old friend the doctor and have long talks with him in his surgery, from which she would come away blowing her nose and very red about the eyelids. She got him to drop in as if by accident every now and then at the manor-house when Tim was at home, and so accustomed was the boy to these half friendly, half professional visits of his earliest friend that she thought they awoke no suspicions in his breast. It was after one of these unofficial inspections that the old doctor delivered himself of the above remark.

'That's what you always said,' replied Mrs. Quitchett; 'I must say you have always said the same; but he seems somehow different this winter from what I've ever seen him before.'

'Do you think,' asked the doctor, 'that he can have anything on his mind? Anything like fretting would be the worst thing in the world for him. I suppose,' he added tentatively, 'he can't have got into any trouble of any kind?'

'Trouble!' echoed Mrs. Quitchett scornfully; 'he's the best-behaved and steadiest boy in the kingdom of Britain. *He* in any trouble; why, a saint from heaven would be more likely ever to have a thought that wasn't out of the Bible than him. As to his having anything on his mind, what *should* he have, poor lamb, I should like to know?'

The doctor said if *she* didn't know of anything, *he* certainly couldn't be expected to; that he had only thrown out the suggestion for what it was worth. Boys would be boys, and the best of them got into scrapes sometimes, and therewith took himself off.

But his nurse was wrong in supposing that the doctor's frequent droppings-in were lost upon Tim. I don't know otherwise what train of thought it could have been which led him one day to ask his father whether his grandmother hadn't died rather suddenly. The question surprised Mr. Ebbesley, who wondered how the boy knew anything about his grandparents.

'Yes,' he said, 'she died very suddenly.'

'Had she heart disease?'

'No. I don't think she had anything of that sort, but she had never been very strong; it was more a general lowness of tone, something like breaking up, and yet she was not an old woman. I think being in that weak state she must have caught something, but I remember very little about it. I was quite a child at the time.'

'Then she was quite young when she died?'

'Oh yes, not thirty, I think; all my mother's family were delicate; they were not long-lived people.' And Mr. Ebbesley rather hastily changed the conversation. This curiosity as to illness and death seemed to him morbid and unhealthy, and perhaps he feared the boy might go on by a natural transition to ask about his own mother.

He had been even less at home than usual that winter, but he too had noticed in his visits to the manor-house that his son was not looking well, and this conversation, chiming in with certain dark hints of Mrs. Quitchett's, made him feel it a duty to have him thoroughly examined before sending him back to school. The Granthurst doctor was sent for in addition to our old friend, and the two together undressed Tim, and sounded him, and thumped him, and did all the inscrutable things doctors do. 'No,' they said, 'there was no organic trouble. The lungs were not affected; the action of the heart was weak, but not in any way diseased; the general tone was low; the circulation bad. He must not overtire himself, must be made to dress warm, must be well fed,' etc. etc. etc. So Tim went back to Eton with many injunctions from Mrs. Quitchett, who was more than usually fussy and particular in her directions to him, to be very careful not to get tired or to sit in damp clothes, and to be sure to put something round his neck and over his mouth if he had to go out at night.

Tim was sixteen that March. How our story runs away with us, carrying us over years in which he changed much in many ways, but remained always unchanged on the side on which my business is to show him. He had been growing a good deal of late, yet he was not tall for his age either, and his slight, graceful figure made him look younger than he really was. His hands too were small—delicate slender hands with long fingers, such as do not often belong to boys who are quite strong. Tommy

Weston, who had a very respectable-sized fist, used to chaff him about them, and solemnly invent receipts for the widening of them, which Tim took in very good part, having a great regard for Tommy, and not caring a brass farthing about his hands. It was bitter cold at Eton that fives half, and Tim, despite his warm clothes, was chilly, and had to stay out several times.

But Easter came at last, mild, sweet, and smiling, as so often happens after a cold winter. Easter was late that year, and the cuckoo was calling from tree to tree and wildflowers blowing in field and hedgerow when Tim came home again. He was just a little whiter, a little thinner, nothing very noticeable, yet Mrs. Quitchett noticed it, and the doctor's words spoken so many years before came back to her kind old mind: 'Things will affect him more than other people all his life; what would be nothing to an ordinary person might kill him.' She remembered too his question as to whether the boy could have anything on his mind.

'Do you feel ill, my dearie?' she asked him.

'Oh no, thanks, nurse dear,' he answered. 'You all make such a fuss over me that you will end by making me think there is something really the matter.'

'Tim, my lamb,' asked the old woman earnestly, 'you won't mind if I ask you a question? — remember it's your old nurse, who loves you better than any one else, and don't be angry, — you haven't, not by your own fault I know, but out of kindness or anything, you haven't got into any trouble at school, have you?'

'Why, what put that into your head?' asked Tim, and being tickled with the idea, he laughed so heartily that Mrs. Quitchett was reassured on *that* head.

Still she persisted. 'There isn't anything, then, that's troubling you, is there, dear, — nothing on your mind, as you may say?'

This time Tim did not laugh; he looked at her with some surprise, but he only said, 'You dear silly old goose, what *should* I have on my mind?' and kissed her, and so the matter dropped.

But Mrs. Quitchett and the doctor were not so far wrong after all; say what he would, Tim's illness was partly mental. The cloud of his father's displeasure, unexpressed yet always present, shadowed his whole life. Thus his greatest joy, his friendship with Carol, came to involve his greatest grief, his alienation from the only parent he had ever known; and the constant conflict of emotions told on the boy's sensitive nature, and reacting on his bodily health, helped to weaken his already too weak constitution. And Carol, meaning only to be kind, contrived, like most well-meaning people, to make matters worse by coming to see him nearly every day. He could talk unrestrainedly to him about Violet, as he could to no one else; besides, he too had noticed the growing pallor and creeping lassitude of Tim, and being really and sincerely fond of his friend, began to grow anxious about him. He rarely encountered Mr. Ebbesley, and certainly never guessed at his objecting to his intimacy with his son. When they met, the older man was always studiously polite to the younger; if he was rather cold too, it was not very noticeable, Mr. Ebbesley's manner to the general public not being chiefly remarkable for warmth or geniality. Tim, however, lived on thorns; he had made his choice and would stick to it, but he was particularly anxious to avoid doing anything that could look like an act of open defiance, and all this perpetual flourishing of Carol about the place might very easily, in his father's eyes, be made to bear such an interpretation. Every time the two met he underwent real suffering, such as no one can understand who has not experienced something like it. Mrs. Quitchett, noting the shade that crossed her master's face, and the quick flush and drooping of the eyelids with which Tim mentioned Carol's name every time circumstances obliged him to do so in his father's presence, or rather, perhaps, guided by that divine intuition which lends a sort of second sight to those who love much, arrived at some glimmering suspicion of the state of affairs. The doctor's suggestion of Tim's having some secret cause of worry had set her mind all agog to discover and if possible remove it; and Mr. Ebbesley's strange behaviour on the day of his return from India recurred suddenly to her recollection, and seemed to supply the clue to all this mystery which her cross-questioning had failed to extract from Tim. Now as then her love made her bold, and she determined to attack her master on the subject the next time he came to Stoke Ashton. She had carried her point then, and might again; the only thing that troubled her resolution was an embarrassing doubt of what the point precisely was that she desired to carry. Then she had a definite thing to try for; she wished to extract permission for Carol to come to the manor-house, and had succeeded in doing so. But here was Carol coming there every day, more than he had ever done before. What she was to ask, she knew not; but she felt, as she would have expressed it, 'that she would be guided to speak' when the time came, and she resolved to make the attempt for her boy's sake.

'If you please, sir, can I speak to you a minute?' she asked, planting herself in the lion's path on the first opportunity that presented itself. She felt that what she was going to say bordered on impertinence, and her heart quaked, though her face was calm.

'Certainly, nurse,' answered Mr. Ebbesley with grave affability; 'is it about the books? Do you want some money?'

'Not at present, thank you, sir; the fact is, I want to speak to you about your son.'

Mr. Ebbesley looked up quickly, but said nothing.

'Do you think that boy looks well?' inquired Mrs. Quitchett impressively.

'He certainly does not look as well as I should like to see him,' admitted the other rather unwillingly, 'but he never has done that. As to his *being* ill, I can't find out that there is anything the matter with him; he has been very thoroughly examined by the doctors. Is there anything else you can suggest?'

'Shall I tell you what the doctor asked *me*?' asked the nurse, still with the air of Nemesis.

'Certainly; let me hear it, though I don't suppose he is likely to have said anything different to you from what he did to me.'

'He asked me,' continued the old lady, 'if the boy had anything on his mind, if he was worried about anything.'

Mr. Ebbesley started. The conversation was taking a turn he by no means expected.

'What in the world should a child like that have to be worried about?' he asked rather testily.

Mrs. Quitchett did not flinch.

'If you'll excuse the liberty I'm taking,' she said, 'I think I can tell you, sir. I may be wrong, for I am only an ignorant old woman; but when anything ails that boy I'm just bound to try and find it out; and I think I have.'

'For Heaven's sake say out what you mean!' exclaimed Mr. Ebbesley crossly; 'if there's anything you want me to do, tell me what it is.'

'That boy's fretting, I can see plainly; and it's something to do with you and young Mr. Darley, though I don't know what.'

Mr. Ebbesley jumped out of his chair with a smothered execration, and began to walk about the room.

'Has my son been complaining of me to you?' he asked presently.

Mrs. Quitchett smiled with fine scorn, not untouched by pity, for the poor man who understood his own child so little.

'Not he,' she answered laconically; 'I haven't so much as got one word out of him about it, though I've tried; but he frets — any one may see that. And I'm very much mistaken if that's not what it's about.'

'What do you wish me to do?' asked Mr. Ebbesley, sitting down again and putting on his grand manner. 'Does not my son have perfect liberty to see his friend as much as he wishes? Do I interfere in any way?'

'I can't say as you do, sir,' answered Mrs. Quitchett thoughtfully, 'and that's just what puzzles me. The young man he come and go as he likes, but your son's not at ease about it; and I notice that he never mentions his friend to you if he can possibly help it. You know you took a dislike to that boy from the first day you came home and found him here; and whether you've ever said so to your son or not, he know it, and he fret.'

When Mrs. Quitchett felt strongly she had a way of clipping the final s from the third person singular of her verbs, which lent a curious impressiveness to her remarks. There was something so sternly judicial in the old lady's attitude and manner that Mr. Ebbesley felt called upon to make a defence of himself. It seemed as though certain uncomfortable doubts as to his own conduct, which had begun to trouble him of late, had suddenly taken voice and shape and stood up to confront him; and the necessity of justification that he felt addressed itself rather to them than to his visible interlocutor.

'It is true,' he said after a while, 'that I have disapproved of Tim's foolish infatuation for his young neighbour, and I have on one occasion spoken to him about it. He has an unhappy trick of exaggerating trifles, and in the present case has chosen to make a mountain out of a molehill, as usual. I told him that I thought he might with advantage to himself be less like a silly schoolgirl in his friendship and more like a man, and that I thought it bad for him mentally and physically to sit cramped up all day writing long sentimental letters. He chose to talk a great deal of nonsense about not "giving up his friend," and all that kind of thing; and now he is playing at being the persecuted victim, who bears ill-usage heroically for his friend's sake. It is all on a par with the rest. He likes to fancy himself the hero of a story. It's all damn nonsense,' he concluded suddenly, with a rapid drop into irritability.

Mrs. Quitchett was routed; she could say no more. She felt that she had failed; though in other respects she hardly understood Mr. Ebbesley's explanation, that point at least was quite clear to her, and she began to make a sort of apology, 'if she had presumed.'

Her antagonist, feeling pleased with his own exposition of the matter, graciously told her not to distress herself, and added, 'I am quite right, you may be sure, and, I need not say, am acting solely for what I consider to be the boy's own good. I have no personal dislike to young Darley; quite the reverse. I am sure I am right, and some day or other, when he has come to his senses, Tim will be the first to acknowledge it.'

'If he don't die in finding it out,' muttered Mrs. Quitchett as she left the room; but Mr. Ebbesley apparently did not catch what she said.

Now Mr. Ebbesley was not alone in objecting to the intimacy between the lads.

Miss Violet Markham Willis had on several occasions, when she had expressed her sovereign will and pleasure that Carol should do this or that, been met by the answer that he must go and see Tim, who, he was sure, was not well, and who must be dreadfully lonely and blue all by himself in that old frog-hole of a manor-house. Carol in so doing was performing an act of highest self-abnegation, and never doubted that Violet must know it to be such, and approve of his motive. And she, with the odd perversity of young ladies in love, never hinted that she did nothing of the kind. But it is one thing voluntarily to sacrifice oneself to a sense of duty, and quite another to be sacrificed, without one's consent, to some one else's sense of duty. *She* had never shot Tim with a gun, and afterwards amused his slow convalescence, or delivered him from stoning, or loftily received his admiring devotion for eight years; consequently it was not to be expected that she should in any way share Carol's feeling about him; and to her he seemed only a most uninteresting and unnecessary little person, who was constantly interfering between her and her legitimate property. As a consequence of all which, Carol's amiability struck her as overdone, and she was decidedly inclined to dislike the unhappy object of it.

Now it happened at this time that Mrs. Markham Willis gave her hard-worked governess a holiday, the first for two years, and Violet undertook to rule the schoolroom in her absence. The little Markham Willises were what is called lively, high-spirited children, and finding the yoke off their necks, they became pretty nearly unmanageable, and gave their elder sister a great deal of trouble. Violet was a very good girl in her way, but by no means a saint; she liked to enjoy herself, and to have her own way, and to be a good deal petted and flattered, and told how nice and how pretty she was; and this severe and unusual strain on her patience proved a little too much for her temper. She had undertaken this, being really anxious to be of use to her mother, and from the best of motives, and she was determined to go through with it and not complain, but she was having a rough time of it; and, moreover, it galled her pride to have to acknowledge that she could not keep the order that seemed to result as though by magic from the mere presence of the meek, colourless Fräulein, whom in her heart she had always rather looked down upon. She felt sick and cross and bitter, and as some one else always has to suffer when any one is in that frame of mind, poor Carol came in for trouble in the present instance as being the handiest and likeliest person on whom to vent her displeasure.

It is far oftener for some one else's faults than for our own that we receive chastisement at the hands of our friends and relatives, and for the most part we do not even know whose sins it is that we are bearing vicariously. Maggie Tulliver had an old wooden doll that she ground and beat when impotently hating her fellow-creatures, and Violet pitched upon her lover to act this uncomfortable part. Perhaps their true love had run a little too smooth if anything, and with human unreasonableness, she may have felt that a little breeze in that direction might clear the air and infuse the proper amount of necessary excitement into the long wooing, which threatened to become a trifle prosaic. Anyhow it is certain that Carol was made to suffer. And when anything ailed Carol, Tim, you may be sure, was not long in finding it out. He noticed that his friend came in and sat down wearily, asking how he was in a sort of perfunctory manner, as one whose mind was elsewhere. (Ordinarily Carol's advent was made known by shouts or singing long before he entered the house.) He walked about aimlessly and stared out of window, much as he had done on that memorable day at Eton. Tim forbore to press for confidences until Carol felt inclined to make them; indeed, he almost hoped he would make none; he felt trouble in the air by a sort of instinct, and shrank from fresh burthens, with sheer physical weakness. Carol could talk of nothing, settle to nothing, and soon went away; he was manifestly distressed about something. Again, the next day, he was even more dejected, and on the third he broke silence.

'I've been poor company these last few days,' he said with a sudden effort, 'but I've been thinking of my own affairs, I'm afraid, and not of you at all. The fact is I'm infernally miserable, and you must try not to mind me.'

'You miserable! Oh, Carol, why didn't you say so sooner? Can I do anything for you? Do tell me what's the matter.'

'There! I knew I should make you wretched; I'm a selfish brute to come and make you unhappy too; but I can't help it. I've tried to say nothing about it.'

'And do you suppose,' asked Tim reproachfully, 'that I haven't seen that something was wrong? How blind you must think me; or else that I care very little about you, not to have noticed.'

'I suppose I ought to have stayed away,' said poor Carol dejectedly. 'I'm not fit company for a dog when I'm out o' spirits, but I try to keep cheery at home for the sake of the dear old people; and it's such a comfort to give up every now and then, and look as gloomy as one feels. I'm a bad hand at pretending; indeed, I've never had to before.'

'You need not trouble to with *me*, at least,' said Tim, smiling faintly; 'I know you far too well not to see through it in a minute. But all this time you haven't told me what's the matter.'

Carol blushed hotly. 'Violet—' he stammered, and then stopped abruptly.

'Oh, Carol!' Tim exclaimed, aghast, 'you don't mean to say she—' The thought was too awful to be put into words, but Carol answered it.

'No; not exactly,' he admitted moodily; 'not in so many words, but that's what it's coming to, I can see.'

And then he went on to tell how Violet's manner had changed to him of late. She was no longer as she once was, but more as though he had offended her somehow, and yet he could think of nothing he had done. No, clearly it was not *his* fault; she had got tired of him, that was all, and meant to throw him over; it was very natural, and he had been a fool to expect anything else. She was a great deal too good for him, and he couldn't blame her. Had not he himself refused to bind her? She had been too young to know her own mind, and had seen so few people; he supposed she'd seen some other fellow she liked better—and the poor boy ground his teeth at the bare thought. She had a perfect right to do as she liked, and it was good of her to let him down easy; anyway he must try and take it like a man, and not make a fool of himself.

On another occasion he broke down altogether. 'Violet,' he said, 'had shown her coldness towards him in the most marked way; he had seen her coming down the road alone, and had hurried forward, determined at all risks to ask what had changed her towards him,—any certainty, even the worst, would be better than this suspense. But when she saw him, she had turned down a lane obviously to avoid him, and he had not had the heart to follow her.' The poor fellow looked almost as pale as Tim, and actually burst out crying when he came to this point in his narrative. It was the first time in all their long intercourse that Tim had ever seen Carol cry, and the act seemed so utterly foreign to his hero, and out of keeping in every way, that it filled him with dismay, and took from him all power of comfort or reasoning.

'Oh, Carol! oh, dear *dear* Carol! please don't,' was all he could say; the sight of tears in those eyes was more than he could stand.

He could only accompany him home, giving him the help of his sympathetic silence, and wisely refraining from all attempts at speech.

'Thanks, dear old boy,' Carol said as he wrung his hand at parting; 'you've done me lots of good'; and Tim went away alone for a little stroll through the woods to ponder on all this network of trouble. Things too deep for his comprehension seemed to be closing in upon him. That *he* should be unhappy had come to appear to him more or less in the natural order of things; but Carol!

What manner of creature then was this girl who could so sway the first of men? To what order of beings did she belong, who might have Carol for her very own, and exist in perpetual happiness with him, in perfect interchange of affection, no one blaming or thwarting her; who yet treated him like this and made him wretched? Many possibilities had suggested themselves to Tim, but never this one. He was confused; his head ached with thinking. The cheerful sights and sounds of the wood, now beginning to deck itself with its first green, the bustle of the birds at their early nest-building, the delicate yellow of the primroses gemming the ground all about his feet, which at another time would have been lovingly noted by him, had to-day no message of comfort for the puzzled boy, as he vainly tried to find the ends of these tangled threads of life, and love, sorrow, and anger.

Presently his path led him out of the wood into a little parklike strip of meadowland, skirting the lane that would take him home. The boundary hedge was set on a bank sloping gently this way and that, but the meadow was on a higher level than the lane. It was a balmy soft afternoon, unusually mild for the time of year, and Tim was rather tired with his walk; the thought just crossed his mind, how much more easily tired he seemed to be now than formerly, as he sat down on the soft moss and leaned his head against the trunk of a large tree that grew on the summit of the bank, jutting out from the hedge on either side. How long he sat there he did not know; he must have fallen into a kind of unconsciousness, for he did not think he was asleep.

He was roused at length by a sound of voices, and peeping through the hedge he could discern the tops of two feminine hats, whose wearers had evidently seated themselves on the lane side of the bank to rest, directly below where he was. He was rising to pass on, when his attention was attracted by the mention of his own name and that of Carol, in a voice that made him thrill; it was Violet Markham Willis who was speaking. He could not go on now; his legs refused their office, and he sank down again in the same place. With instinctive repulsion from the meanness of eavesdropping, he tried to call out to warn her that he was there but no sound came from his lips. He was as though paralysed, yet with all his senses morbidly acute; and then his whole being seemed to resolve itself into an imperious necessity not to lose a word of this conversation.

Violet spoke in a high aggrieved tone, not difficult to catch in the stillness of the spring evening. Mrs. Markham Willis had made some remark on her daughter's altered looks and manner of late, and Violet, concealing the schoolroom troubles, had laid the blame on Carol, whereupon her mother had said a word of expostulation on that head too.

'Oh, Carol!' the girl was saying, when her voice first struck Tim's ear.

'Carol doesn't care two straws about me; he may have fancied himself in love with me at first, but it's easy to see he's tired of me. Would he be perpetually running after that nasty little Ebbesley friend of his, if he were really fond of me? he's always with him, far more than he is with me, I'm sure.'

'Dearest Violet,' her mother answered, 'are you not a little unreasonable? I can't see, I'm sure, what Carol finds so attractive in that boy, though I fancy it is his kindness. The poor fellow is delicate, and very fond of him; and after all, he has a right to choose his own friends.'

'I should be the last to wish to deny it to him,' Violet retorted defiantly; 'he can make a free choice; if he prefers "Tim," as he calls him, to me, let him have his choice by all means.' And rather inconsistently with her brave words, she began to cry. She was wrought up and nervous, anxious to make something appear like a tangible grievance.

'Oh, my darling, consider,' cried Mrs. Markham Willis; 'are you not trifling with your own happiness? I am sure Carol loves you very much, poor fellow; and you know it too, if it were not for this foolish misunderstanding. Tell me, dear, what makes you think he cares so much for this friend?'

'What makes me think!' echoed Violet, sobbing. 'Doesn't he always say he must go to him, if I suggest our doing anything together? Isn't he for ever talking about him, and making him an excuse to get away from me? If he wants me to play second fiddle to that ridiculous boy, he's just mistaken; I'll never marry a man with an intimate friend. Never.'

'Dear dear Violet! don't talk so loud; some one is coming. Oh! don't cry, darling; do dry your eyes. I wouldn't have any one see you crying here in the public lane for worlds. Have some self-respect, for my sake if not for your own. Oh! dear, come quick; your eyes are quite red, and you have no veil; and some one really *is* coming.'

So this was the conclusion, the explanation of the whole matter. It was he, Tim, that was the bar to the happiness of the one being he loved more than all the world. There was an irony in it all that made it hard, very hard. There are moments in which thought gallops with us, and Tim's resolve was taken so quickly that he wondered at himself. Not for an instant did he waver, nor rejoice that if he would, he could keep his friend to himself. Even the thought that Carol cared enough for him to make the girl to whom he was virtually engaged suppose that she held only a secondary place in his affections, could not shake his purpose. His duties all pointed one way — that to his father and that to his friend brought into sudden harmony in a way he had little looked for. Yes, duties pointed one way, but feelings tugged the other; and though resolved to follow duty, he had a hard struggle to quiet the turmoil within him. He walked home very slowly, strengthening himself in his purpose. 'Nothing ever shall,' Carol had said; 'at least it will be your fault if it does.' How well he remembered the words, and his own scorn of such an impossibility. Now they mocked his wretchedness, and with them recurred another sentence from quite a different conversation. His own words to his father seemed to rise in judgment against him, and he did not try to appeal from them. 'If one loved a person truly, one would do anything for him, even give him up.' He was determined that he would never repay all Carol's kindness by ruining his life for him. He did not pause to think of what he was doing to his own; that was a side of the question on which he found it safer not to dwell at present

When he reached home he went straight to the room where he knew he should find his father. Going up to him, he said, 'Do you remember our talk about Carol Darley, just a year ago?' He spoke low and quickly, holding his hat in one hand and supporting himself at the table with the other.

Mr. Ebbesley could not help a hasty questioning look; he was taken by surprise; but he answered coldly, 'Perfectly; I am not likely to forget. You were good enough on that occasion to inform me that you preferred that young gentleman to me, and that you intended deliberately to disobey my express desires, which I must say you have done most thoroughly.'

'It was the first time I ever disobeyed you, and you don't know what it cost me; but that is not the point. Since then I have thought it over; I am come to say that I will do as you wish.'

Mr. Ebbesley was more surprised than ever, but he would have died rather than show it. He only said, 'I am glad to hear it; I don't ask what has brought you to your senses at last; I suppose you have had a quarrel.'

But Tim did not answer; his heart was too full. He was wrought to the utmost pitch of endurance of which he was capable. He could not have said another word to save his soul. He hurried almost stumbling from the room; the necessity to be alone was strong upon him.

CHAPTER XII

But sworn I have; and never must
Your banished servant trouble you;
For if I do, you may mistrust
The vow I made to love you, too.

Herrick.

The next time Carol came to the manor-house Tim was not to be found;
he had run and hidden himself in the garden when he saw him coming.
Crouching among the bushes, he could hear the dearly-loved voice calling him by the familiar nickname, and his courage nearly gave out; he
pressed his hands over his mouth as though he would choke back the
answering cry that rose naturally to his lips.

'Tim, Tim!' shouted Carol, 'where are you?'

Either there was, or Tim fancied there was, a tone of disappointment
in the voice. Carol was in trouble; Carol had need of him, and he must
hear him call and let him go unsatisfied away. It was his free act too; no
one had compelled him to it. But it was for Carol's own sake; and in that
thought alone he was strong.

For weeks afterwards, in the silence of the night, whenever he lay
awake (and he lay awake a good deal in those nights), he heard that voice
calling to him, 'Tim, Tim!' in saddest accents of one that sought something
on which he had counted, and found it not. He felt that his one chance lay
in avoiding a meeting with Carol, and the constant watch and care to do
so told on him fearfully, making him nervous and excitable. He dreaded
to stay at home, lest his friend should come and see him, and almost more
to go out, lest he should come upon him unawares. He could settle to
nothing; every step on the path, every voice, every opening door, made
him start and tremble, and when he could stand it no longer, and seized
his hat to rush out no matter where, he would be taken with such an
agony of apprehension before he had gone a hundred yards, that he had
scarcely strength to get back to the house. No one will ever know what he
suffered in those few days; and when his father, taking pity on his altered
looks, offered to take him to the seaside till it should be time for him to return to Eton, he eagerly accepted. Not a word was spoken between them
about Carol; the subject was avoided by tacit consent. William Ebbesley
wondered not a little what had influenced his son to act as he had done,
but he would not ask. He had long given up trying to understand the boy,

who was as full of incomprehensible moods as a woman. He concluded that deference to his wishes had not had a large share in determining him, but there he did Tim injustice. Anyway his point was gained, and he could afford to be magnanimous; so the two went off to the sea together for the remaining week or ten days of Tim's holidays.

Poor Carol failed utterly at first to understand what had happened. Tim was never to be found when he went to the manor-house, never came to the Court. Then one day the answer to his inquiry was that Mr. Ebbesley and Tim were gone away to the seaside together. Tim was 'poorly,' the little maid who trembled under Mrs. Quitchett told him, 'needed change of air, the doctor had said.'

'And had he left no message for him?' Carol asked; 'was she sure there was none?'

Yes; the little maid thought she was sure there was none. Mrs. Quitchett was out, but she would ask her when she came in.

Carol went away sad at heart. Tim would write, he told himself,— was sure to write. He would not yet believe that Tim could mean anything. He was not well; he had had to go away suddenly; he would be sure to write in a day or two. So he waited the day or two, but still Tim made no sign. Then Carol got the address from Mrs. Quitchett, and wrote himself, but no answer came back. He began to grow anxious after that; to imagine all sorts of possibilities; he had not known how fond he was of his friend. He determined to go again to the manor-house, and ask if the accounts of Tim were good.

'Yes'; Mrs. Quitchett 'thanked him; she had had a letter from him that morning, and he said he was better. He liked the sea, and thought it was doing him good.'

'And was there any—any message or anything? in short, anything about *me* in the letter?' Carol asked with a little proud hesitation.

No, there was nothing; Mrs. Quitchett had noticed it and thought it strange. 'But doubtless he means to write you a long letter himself one of these days,' said the good-natured old woman; 'he knew his old nurse would be anxious, God bless him! and so he wrote to her first.'

But the letter Mrs. Quitchett predicted never came. 'If he is well enough to write to her,' Carol thought, 'he is surely up to sending me just a line, if only to say how he is; he might know I should be anxious.' And he felt, not unnaturally, a little hurt. He would not write again until Tim chose to answer his first letter, which had been all a kindly affectionate heart could make it, sympathy for his ill-health, regret at his going, and no hint of blame at the manner of it, not a word about himself. He had done what he could; now he would wait.

These were sad times for Carol; he was so unused to sorrow that it had all the added weight of strangeness. Violet seemed to have given him up, and now Tim—Tim, to whom he had turned in his grief with such implicit reliance,—just when most he needed the support of friendship and kindness, Tim had thrown him over too.

'I bored him with my troubles,' said the poor boy to himself a little bitterly; 'it was very natural; one could not expect a child like that to feel interest in such a subject. And yet he *seemed* so fond of me, and he never was quite like other boys of his age—older and younger at once, somehow. Well, well, who would have thought he was only a fair-weather friend after all!'

He did not know, poor fellow, all that the 'fair-weather friend' had borne, and was bearing, for his sake; he could not see him sitting gazing out to sea hour after hour, with eyes that saw nothing, and ears to which the long wash of the waves upon the beach kept always calling 'Tim, Tim!' in the never-to-be-forgotten tones that he had heard but the other day in the old manor-house garden.

But when things are at their worst they generally mend, and Carol presently found a star rising on his night, that promised to comfort him not a little. It was about this time that Miss Markham Willis, finding that *the rôle* she had assumed was anything but an easy or pleasant one, finding too that the obnoxious Tim had gone away, and seeing that Carol looked delightfully miserable as he made her a fine sarcastic bow when they occasionally met in their walks or rides, began wisely to consider that it did not make her domestic worries easier to bear to cut herself off from her principal extraneous source of enjoyment, and so determined to take pity on her lover, and show him some signs of kindness. At first these only took the form of a few gracious smiles. Then finding that these had not quite the effect she desired, she made her mother take her to call at the Court, and there, as she had hoped, was Carol.

'Why, Lily dear,—I mean Violet!' cried old Mrs. Darley, 'I declare you are quite a stranger; where have you hidden yourself all these days?'

'Oh! there has been so much to do at home, dear Mrs. Darley,' answered Violet, all radiant with smiles, and glowing on Carol at secondhand through grandmamma. 'You know Fräulein has gone away for a holiday, so I have all the children on my hands from morning till night. I never appreciated poor Fräulein before; but now I have had a taste of what her life is, I feel quite differently towards her; if it was only the bread-and-butter. I assure you, I rival Goethe's Charlotte in the art of cutting bread-and-butter.'

'Dear, dear, do young folks read the sorrows of What's-his-name nowadays? My poor dear mother never would allow us to. She said it was a dreadful book, and that when it first came out it made all the young men commit suicide. To tell the truth, when I did read it, I didn't think it very interesting, but perhaps I am not a good judge. You *do* take sugar, Mrs. Wilkins, don't you?'

'Please yes, a little; thank you, quite enough. I *do* hope, Mrs. Darley, I haven't let Violet read anything improper; what you said just now about that book, you know. But Fräulein told me all young ladies read it in Germany as being a classic. I don't read German myself, but I placed reliance on her.'

Carol meanwhile held obstinately in the background, looking black as a thunder-cloud, and strongly inclined to compare himself with the other unfortunate who was cursed with love for a woman that cut bread-and-butter. But when the visitors rose to take leave, while the elders were making their little farewell speeches, Violet took occasion to say to him in an undertone, and with a look of gentlest expostulation—

'Are you angry with me, Carol? you haven't been to see us for an age; won't you come and see us again?'

Had he been dreaming? he wondered; was it all a mistake of his, this fancied coldness on her part? She spoke with such entire innocence, a little justly hurt, but ready to forgive, that he began to think it must have been his fault. His resentment was not proof against this; he pressed the little hand she held out to him, and promised to come next day.

'I am going primrosing in the morning.' she said, 'in Fern Dingle, so it is no good coming then.'

And on the way home she seemed in such high spirits, that her mother stole her hand into hers and asked her what she had said to Carol. But Violet for all answer trilled out the words of an old catch—

The falling out of faithful friends, renewal is of love,

until the woods echoed to her bright clear singing; and then, putting her arm round her mother, she said, 'Silly mamma,' and kissed her.

Of course Carol vowed to himself that nothing should tempt him to go near Fern Dingle the next morning, and of course he went; and there, over the big half-filled basket of primroses, the lovers made up this not very terrible quarrel. Violet was half contrite, half reproachful, wholly gentle and charming.

'Had she been sulky? she half feared so; but she had been dreadfully busy, and the children had been a little tiresome sometimes, and she had been rather out of sorts. Carol must forgive her if she had unwittingly hurt him; how *could* he suppose she meant anything; he ought to have *known* she didn't.'

And Carol, we may be sure, was not very hard to melt. He began, on the contrary, to feel that it was he who was in the wrong for having doubted Violet's constancy; but for this he, in his turn, received absolution, and was presently taken back into favour.

As to Tim, his name was not mentioned between them; if they thought about him at all, which is unlikely, they certainly did not waste these precious moments in talking about him. Violet's little spurt of indignation against him was of the most transitory nature; had she recollected it, it would have been to be rather ashamed of it; besides, he was gone away, and that was enough; and Carol would certainly not have introduced a subject on which he was feeling a little sore. Violet was restored to him; the first cloud that had shadowed his young brightness had rolled away; and nothing else seemed to matter much. He went back to Cambridge in a far more peaceful frame of mind, and plunged with robust cheerfulness into all the pleasures of the May term.

One day the old Squire, meeting Mr. Ebbesley on the road, stopped his pony to ask after Tim.

'Sorry to hear your boy was not quite strong, Ebbesley,' he said kindly.

'Thank you,' said Mr. Ebbesley; 'he is quite well again now, and gone back to school.'

'Ah! I must tell Carol when I write; he'll be glad to hear it; the boys are fond of one another; but most likely the young 'un will be writing to him himself.'

'Ah! by the way, Mr. Darley, that reminds me, if you are writing to your grandson, will you kindly say my boy hopes he will excuse his not writing to him at present? he has to read rather hard for his upper division trials, and by the doctor's advice, I discourage his working his brain in other ways, too.'

'Quite right, quite right. When I was a lad we didn't write letters much. To be sure, it was before the penny post; but I can't say I should have used it much if it had been invented. I never was a good correspondent; I don't think I ever wrote to my poor dear father when I was a lad except when I wanted money, which I generally didn't get. Well, good-bye. Can you come and dine with us, Tuesday?'

'Thank you, but I am obliged to go to town again to-morrow.'

And so the two men separated; and, the Squire's memory not being of the best, Carol never got the message.

It was quite true; Tim was trying very hard to drown in work the recollection of his troubles. It is not easy to take bodily out of one's life a sentiment, the growth of nearly eight years, and not feel the change; and

Tim's was not a nature to which changes came easily. To take his devotion to Carol *out* of his life, did I say? Why, it *was* his life; it had begun when he first began to feel anything, and had grown with his growth ever since. In some fantastic way everything else in the world seemed to cluster round that central point; nothing was of interest until he had somehow brought it into relation with this ruling and pervading sentiment. And it was this that he had undertaken to cast from him and forget. He felt as some flower might which a child had plucked from its root, and then stuck back in the ground expecting it to go on growing as heretofore.

As often happens, after the very cold winter came an unusually hot summer. The air seemed to pulse and vibrate. Scarcely a leaf stirred of the lime-trees before the chapel, heavy and odorous with their wealth of blossom, and drowsy with the hum of innumerable bees. The boys grew languid and listless over their lessons, and even over their games. They fell asleep in three o'clock school, an offence with which the masters could not in their hearts but feel a secret sympathy. The dust seemed to spring eternal, almost from under the very hose of the water-cart that went ceaselessly to and fro through the highways of the old school, and the pelargoniums and fuchsias drooped in the window-boxes, because their owners had not the energy to water them. Eton is a healthy place, in spite of all its enemies say to the contrary, and the life there is for most boys the healthiest that could be devised. But Tim was not as most boys. To him, to eat, sleep, and study in one small room, to wear a high hat and a tight black cloth coat, with the thermometer at something fabulous in the shade, was very trying. The heat that made other lads drowsy and languid, roused him to unnatural and feverish alertness; so far from sleeping in school, he did not sleep at all. When we reflect that in addition to this he was fretting day and night over his hidden sorrow, — a sorrow from which he was persistently trying to find escape in extra hard work, in spite of headaches and other warning signs, — the result is not difficult to foretell. What wonder if he broke down? He never went in for those upper division trials. One day he did not come to dinner, he the soul of regularity; and when they went to look for him they found him stretched on the floor of his room, his face white and set, his eyes open, but with no consciousness in them. They put him to bed and sent for the doctor, who pronounced it a curious case.

'It is no doubt partly the heat,' he said, 'and he has been working too hard; but he must have been in a wretched state of health to begin with; neither the weather nor his work is enough to account for it.'

'He has never been very strong,' answered his tutor, 'and lately I have noticed that he has been working very hard, harder than was necessary even. I have had once or twice to put on the drag, a thing I am very seldom forced to do.'

'He must have perfect rest and quiet, and must not write or read even the lightest books for a long time to come; when he is able to bear the move, he had better be taken home.'

So the tutor went and wrote a kind sympathetic letter to Mr. Ebbesley, telling him his son was ill. How ill he thought him he took care not to say, but he did say enough to carry an awful dread to the father's heart. A chill foreboding seized upon him, and would not be shaken off,—a presentiment that he was to lose his child, that child so zealously longed for, so little appreciated, and yet in a way so deeply loved.

William Ebbesley was in no sense of the word religious; the rough struggle with the world that had filled his early years had not tended to bring him into the devotional attitude, nor had he ever been visited by one of those overwhelming joys that sweep the soul, whatever the nature of its beliefs, with an imperious necessity for giving thanks. And great and terrible as had been some of his sorrows, they had been such as harden and embitter rather than the reverse. But now he felt in some dim way a kind of wonder if this were intended as a punishment to him for the little regard he had paid to the one blessing of his life, which, in that it did not bless him in strict accord with his own notions of what he desired, he had flung from him so carelessly, the priceless gem of his child's love. How that child could love, he had seen; and till now the thought that the love was not for him but another, had chafed and angered him. Now he was humbled by it. Who could say but that had he tried, he might have turned at least some streamlet of those freshening waters into his own parched and rugged field?

There was an old woman once to whom certain kind friends of mine used to send her dinner. She was quite past work, and absolutely destitute, except for what was bestowed upon her in charity, but if the victuals were not to her taste she would send them back. Was it that by so doing she got better ones? On the contrary, the alternative was to fast, and indeed to risk offending the givers, and so cutting herself off from the alms for ever. The proverb that half a loaf is better than no bread, is one to which we all give assent with our lips, but few people, if any, are found willing to make it a rule of conduct. They will have a whole loaf, new and soft, of the finest wheaten flour, and baked just as they choose, or they will eat no bread, though they starve for it. These are perhaps somewhat homely illustrations for the state of mind of a father half wild with grief and self-reproach over a dying son. For something told him, as I have said, that the gift which he had so recklessly cast aside, would never be his now. His boy would die, and would never know how much he really loved him. If he could only win him back to life, only make him think a little more kindly of his father, he felt that nothing else mattered.

He went and fetched Tim home himself, and when he saw how ill and fragile the lad looked, his heart died within him; he longed to fall on his knees by him and tell him how he loved him, and implore him not to leave him. But the doctor had cautioned him to betray no emotion, and to conceal as far as possible any shock he might experience at his son's appearance.

At first for a few days Tim suffered from a raging pain in the head; he could bear no light and no sound, and they feared that he would have brain fever. Then suddenly the pain left him, but left him so exhausted that he hardly seemed alive. Still, weak as he was, the doctor thought he had better be taken away from school, and his father carried him back to the old manor-house where his childhood had past. As though to mock William Ebbesley's grief by violent contrast to the pale and feeble Tim, it was the time of year when the earth is most instinct with buoyant and vibrating life,—July, when the last crowning touch has been put to the long work of spring, while no foreshadowing of the yet distant autumn has fallen on any leaf. The lilies were in their tallest, whitest majesty, the roses blushed and glowed in the old garden, where, a few weeks before, Tim had hidden himself from the voice of his friend.

'I never see such a year, sir,' said the gardener; 'everything is a-doing better than I've ever known it since I've lived here.'

Yes. Everything. Everything but that one blossom for which he would gladly have bartered all the wealth of sunny fruit and folded petals, and on which a frosty hand had been laid in the midst of all the warmth of summer. For Mrs. Quitchett's old friend the doctor, who had known Tim from a baby, did not dare conceal from the poor father his belief that the lad would die. How soon he could not say; he might even be wrong, and Tim might take a turn and begin to gain strength; but he was afraid to hope it. The little stock of life in him seemed to be ebbing away. He might go on for a year, or it might be much sooner; it was impossible to say.

'And could nothing be done?' asked the father. 'Were there no new remedies he could try, no learned men to consult, no places or climates in which the flickering young life would have a better chance to reassert itself?'

The old doctor's voice trembled as he answered. He was almost as fond of the child himself, and he grasped Mr. Ebbesley's hand and spoke very gently. 'I should only be deceiving you if I said "yes"; of course consult any one you will, if it will be any comfort to you; but they will only say the same thing. There is no organic disease; he is dying of sheer weakness, and to drag him about the world will only use up the little stock of strength he has left. If, as God grant, he takes a turn and lives till the winter, then I don't say but it would be well to try a better climate. But at present he is as well off here as anywhere.'

So, then, there was no help for it; nothing to do but to watch his child fade slowly from him, to see him grow whiter, thinner, more easily tired day by day.

The Darleys were all away, and Violet was with them. The Court was shut up, and Tim might have wandered up there without any fear of meeting Carol. But he found, when he tried it, that even this walk, short as it was, was beyond his powers, and this, coming upon him with a vague surprise, was the first intimation to him of how ill he really was. He thought of the old childish days when he had skimmed across the fields for miles round his home, and the Court woods had been but the beginning of his rambles.

Mrs. Quitchett thought of those days too, and wept when she compared the child, small and frail, it is true, but lithe and active as a young squirrel, with the figure of the slim lad of sixteen that moved so slowly round the garden paths. 'Who would ha' thought, who would ha' thought that see'd us two,' sobbed the poor old woman, 'that he was the one the Lord would take first to Himself!' But to Tim she showed a smiling front, watching every sign, indefatigable in her zeal to miss no attention that might do good, and never admitting for a moment that he was not getting better.

As the Ethiopian cannot change his skin, so was it not given to William Ebbesley in an instant to alter his whole nature; such changes do not happen in real life; and even now he caught himself sometimes speaking half-sharply to Tim, when the struggle within him was almost more than he could bear. But the boy did not feel afraid of him any longer; it seemed as though he had some intuition of all that his father was suffering and had suffered on his account; he was beginning to understand him, and in the place of his old fear there welled up in his heart an infinite pity.

One day, when Mr. Ebbesley had brought out cushions with which to make the garden seat easy and soft for him, and was turning to go, as he usually did after shyly proffering some such little act of tenderness, Tim laid one of his thin white hands on his, saying, 'You are very good to me, father.'

'Oh! my boy, my little son,' burst out the poor man, 'I have been a very hard father to you. I see it all now; I thought, I meant to do what was right, but I have been very cruel. Oh! if I could only atone! but you will never forgive me, never love me now.'

The cry that had been stifling him was uttered at last, the proud man had humbled himself, the thin partition that for eight years had kept these two apart had crumbled and let them find one another.

Tim for all answer put up his other arm and drew his father's head down upon his breast, and so for a little space they sat quite silent. After a time Tim said very simply, 'Do you remember the talk we had about my grandmother? You said all her family died young; I think *I* shall die this summer.'

His father could not speak: he could not contradict him, he could only fold him more closely in his arms; and it was Tim who spoke again.

'You mustn't fret for me, father; I am surprised myself to find how little I mind the thought; I think I am rather glad. But there is something I have wanted to say. I am afraid I have not been all you wished; I have disappointed and vexed you. Do you forgive me?'

Still his father could not trust himself to answer save by that convulsive hold; the words meant to ask pardon set themselves in array against him like accusing angels. What words could he find strong enough to express all he was feeling? But Tim smiled and was satisfied. He seemed as though he understood.

CHAPTER XIII

... Even the weariest river
Winds, somewhere, safe to sea.

Swinburne's *Garden of Proserpine.*

As the weeks succeeded each other, one thought was ever present in the mind of Tim. 'Shall I see him again before I die? It can do him no harm now. I shall so soon be out of the way; I cannot come between him and his love any more.'

As his poor hands, whose hold on this world was loosening day by day, grew thinner and more transparent, his face paler, his step slower upon the gravel, his heart yearned ever with a patient longing for just one more sight of the friend to whom his whole life had been true. But he had given the crowning proof of his devotion—renunciation. The arms that should have been upholding him in his last sore struggle, he had himself unclasped; the dear lips and eyes that should even now be smiling on his sick-bed, his own free act had sent far away from him.

'He will never know that I was true to him. I shall never see him again.' Through all the long empty hours this one cry repeats itself in his soul. All the little life that is left to him seems concentrated in this one intense longing for Carol. To see his face, to hear his loved voice again, if only for a moment; to tell him the truth at last; only once, just once, before he died. And yet even now he could not put his thought into words,—could not bring himself to make this last request to his father.

As for Mr. Ebbesley, he too was troubled by one thought which he could not find the courage to speak. He was always with Tim now. It was his arm which supported the boy into the garden where he loved to sit, and back to the house; no tending could have been more loving, more sympathetic. But, as I have said, no one changes his whole nature at a leap, even in the great crises of life; and there was yet one struggle to be made with his pride before perfect ease and confidence could exist between them.

Hour after hour would Tim lie silent and uncomplaining, yearning for Carol, but dreading to endanger the new-found treasure of his father's love; dreading to see the old cloud settle on the face that he was watching, the hard look grow round the mouth, as it was wont to do when in the old days he had been obliged to mention his friend's name.

And William Ebbesley would sit beside him all the while, divining his thoughts, knowing there was one supreme proof of his affection to be given to his son, one sacrifice that he could make for him, one happiness that he could give him, and longing to make the effort, yet ever just kept from it by some strange inexplicable shyness and reserve. For a long time he hoped that Tim would break the silence, would be the first to approach the subject; but at last he saw that that was not to be hoped, and he was half angry with himself for the cowardice that made him wish to shift this burthen to those poor weak shoulders. No. It was clearly for him to take the first step; had he not ardently desired some way of showing his devotion to his son, and when he had it, was it possible that he should hesitate?

So one evening when they had been watching the sunset, which had left a sham glow on Tim's white cheeks, William Ebbesley, holding his son's hand, and with face half-turned away, said suddenly, 'Tim, dear, you have not everything you want; there is one thing I have not done for you.'

There was a real glow in Tim's cheeks now; the sunset light had faded, but in its place an inward radiance, brighter but almost as transient, had spread over the delicate face. Feeling his grasp tighten, his father stole a look at him, and even then a pang shot through him at the thought of the love that had called forth this happy flush at the bare chance of a meeting, the love that was not for him, that might perhaps have been his.

'Oh, father! you mean—' Tim began tremulously, and paused; he dared hardly complete the sentence even in his own mind.

William Ebbesley choked down the last touch of the old jealousy. ' I will write to-night,' he said quietly, answering the other's unspoken thought.

But a new trouble had fallen on Tim. 'Will he come?' he said half to himself; and then, 'Oh yes. If I know him for the kind, generous Carol I think him, he will surely come.'

Then he asked, 'Father, may *I* write?'

'You know, dear boy, the doctor has forbidden you to write a word.'

'Yes, I know; but this will do me good. I shall not be easy unless I may.'

'Won't it do if you dictate to me?'

'No. I must write myself; nothing else will do.'

'Well, if you are sure it will not tire you.' And he went and brought the writing things.

Tim took them eagerly, and was beginning to write, when he stopped suddenly and looked up. 'Father, forgive me; I am selfish. You are sorry at this.'

It was so unexpected, the little impulse of unselfish consideration, that at its contact the last drop of bitterness fell from the father's heart, and in his eyes for the first time for more years than he could remember shone the blessed healing tears to which he had so long been a stranger.

'No, no, my darling,' he faltered hastily; 'whatever makes you happy—I—' then his voice broke, and he could not finish.

'God bless you, dear dear father. I am quite happy now.'

And this was Tim's letter: 'I am very ill, Carol—dying, I think. Dear Carol, if I have seemed ungrateful, can you and will you forgive me? I could explain to you if I had you here, but I can't write. Come to me, Carol dear.—Your loving Tim.'

'Father.'

'Yes, dear.'

'Do you want to see what I have written?'

'No, my boy, no.'

Mr. Ebbesley took the letter and sealed it; then he sent it to the address that he had already got from the servants at the Court.

Whether it was the reaction from the tense longing in which he had been living, or merely that as his strength decreased the change in him grew more apparent, Tim seemed to get worse much more quickly after his letter had gone.

The doctor came and went, shaking his head sadly, and saying, 'It is quicker than I thought.' and despair settled down upon the two watchers by the sick boy.

But still Tim waited day by day for the answer that was to bring peace to his soul. Life was slipping away too fast. 'Oh! come, Carol,' he would whisper, 'or it may be too late; she will surely spare you just for a little.'

Tim had been at home nearly a month now; the blazing July weather had ended in a rather wet August. All around, the harvest lay beaten down by the rain; not the only grain stricken ere it had come to maturity. One evening, after a more than usually dreary day, the clouds had broken, giving place to a gorgeous sunset. Tim had been placed on a sofa in the open window, from which he could watch the purple and crimson and gold, and the delicate green and lilac tints of the western sky; the same sofa on which he had lain eight years before, pondering on his 'angel,' and had seen Carol come in with his offering of grapes.

'Father.'

'Yes, my boy.' He knew too well what question was coming.

'Has the postman been?'

'Yes, dear.'

Alas! no letter. Tim did not even ask, knowing that if there were one, it would be given to him at once. He closed his eyes and lay quite still. His father looked wearily out of the window; he knew what was passing in the lad's mind, and had come to desire the letter almost as much as the sick boy himself.

The air was cool and fresh. The garden was yielding a thousand scents to the soft touch of the summer rain. The setting sun lit little coloured lamps in the large drops that hung from every leaf of the grateful trees and shrubs; the birds kept up a drowsy twittering. A few knowing old blackbirds and thrushes, well aware that the moisture brings out the fine fat worms, were hopping about on the grass-plot in search of their supper. All sounds were strangely distinct that evening.

Hark! what was that? surely a step on the wet gravel; not old Richard the gardener's step. No, it was a young foot that struck the ground lightly, and scrunched stoutly along the little approach to the house. Tim's ears had caught the sound, and he started up from his pillows, his cheeks aflame, his eyes bright and eager, while his heart beat loud and fast. He would know that dear step among a thousand.

He had come—at last, at last!

Mr. Ebbesley stole noiselessly away, with a heavy dull ache in his heart, and I am afraid neither of the friends noticed his absence. In the same room, in the same place, in the same attitudes in which they had met as children, they had come together again.

'Oh, Carol! are you come to me?'

'Oh, my poor dear Tim!'

Carol could say no more. He was shocked at the havoc these few short weeks had wrought. A sacred silence rested between them for a few minutes. Enough for Tim that he was there; no need of words. Carol was the first to speak; his voice was hushed and full of awe.

'I was not with my family when your letter came, dear Tim, and they did not know where to forward it to me, as I was moving about; so I never got it for nearly ten days, or I should have been here long ago.'

'Oh, Carol! how good of you to come. I half thought sometimes— forgive me for doubting you—but I thought you might not come at all— after—after the way I treated you.'

'Don't let's talk of that now, Tim; it's past and gone. I don't want you to explain; I am content not to understand. I remember only the dear good friend of the old days, who is come back to me.'

'But I *must* talk of it, please, Carol; I must tell you how it was. It can do no harm now, and I can't leave you thinking hardly of me, for you know I have not very long to live; something tells me you are come only just in time.'

'Oh! dear dear boy, for God's sake, don't talk like that,' said Carol, with a great lump rising in his throat. 'You are not going to—to—' He felt all the repugnance of the young and strong to face the thought, or say the word.

'To die.' Tim finished the sentence for him quite simply. 'Yes, I think so.'

'No, no; you will get well and strong. You must, for all our sakes.'

Tim smiled and shook his head; it did not seem to him worth while to argue the point; that was not what he wanted to say.

'Never mind,' he said gently, in a way that put the subject aside as unimportant. 'If I had lived I could not have had you with me now. I could never have told you what I am going to tell you. Carol, will you believe me when I say that I never wavered for an instant in my love for you; never loved you better than when I seemed to give you up?' Tim was getting excited, and Carol, fearing it would be bad for him, tried in vain to stop him. 'Oh, Carol! it was for your sake I did it; will you believe me when I tell you all this?'

'For my sake, dear old boy? I don't understand you.' He thought his friend's mind was wandering, but he was very patient and tender with him, humouring him, as one would a sick child.

'She said—I heard her say—that I came between you. You know, Carol, it was when you were so unhappy; and then I saw that I was the cause of it all; and so I determined not to come between you any more; and, indeed, indeed, dear Carol, I would have held my tongue for ever, only there is no more need now. I could not die and leave you thinking ill of me. I suppose I ought to have, but I couldn't do it.'

A new light was breaking in upon Carol.

'And did you do all this for me?' he asked wonderingly. 'Why, Tim, I knew you liked me absurdly, much more than I deserved, but I never dreamt you cared as much for me as that.'

'And you understand now, Carol, don't you, why I didn't answer your dear letter? See, I have it here; it never leaves me.'

'I was a beast and a fool to doubt you, Tim. How could I ever have done it? but it *did* seem as though you must be bored with me and my affairs. And all the time you were doing this for me!'

'Carol, did she mind your coming to me? Tell me I have not made fresh mischief between you?'

'She was very unhappy when I told her how ill you were, and she said, "Oh! go at once to him; I can guess what it would be to be ill and wanting you; and he has been waiting so long already." And then she cried, and said a great deal I did not understand at the time about having been jealous of my friendship for you, and having had hard thoughts of you sometimes, and that she was so ashamed of herself now that you were so ill. I was to be sure and tell you, and to ask if you would ever forgive her.'

'There is nothing to forgive,' Tim answered indifferently.

'But how did you guess.' Carol continued, 'how could you imagine that she felt anything of the sort?'

Then Tim told him all that he had overheard Violet say, only softening it off, and generalising a little with fine tact. And then, the floodgates once open, he went on with sudden eloquence, the more touching from its sheer simplicity, and told all the long story of his constant love, but with as little mention as possible of his father throughout, and of the part he had played in it. And this short hour, which some may think was a sad one, was just the happiest of Tim's whole life.

Carol listened in wonder and awe, not unmingled with compunction, as the description of the feeling he had so unconsciously excited unrolled itself before him. He forgot himself, Violet, his love for her, everything for the moment in contemplation of this devotion, so single-hearted, so lofty, so pure and so unselfish, which had been his, all his, and at which he had been so far from guessing.

'I had no idea of anything of the kind,' he said, more to himself than to Tim. 'I knew the old people were awfully fond of me, God bless them; and I understand what I feel for Violet. But this beats me; I've always been what's called popular, I suppose. I never thought much about it, but fellows have always been jolly to me, and seemed to like me. Oh! my dear friend, what have I ever done that you should care about me like this?'

Tim's face lit up exultingly. '"Passing the love of women,"' he said; 'that was it, Carol, wasn't it? "Thy love to me was wonderful, passing the love of women." Do you remember the day when they read it in the lesson in chapel at Eton?'

Carol had forgotten, but Tim's words brought back the scene with strange distinctness: the big chapel in its stillness, the silence of a great crowd, and of a crowd unused to be still, the little flecks of light from the air-holes in the roof, the ugly picture of the finding of Moses in the window opposite his seat, the droning voice of the reader, and the flash of the little face that turned up to his, with the expression that had puzzled him at the time.

'Yes, I remember,' he answered.

'I have thought of it so often since. It would be grand for one's friend to be able to say that of one, after one was dead. Put your strong arms round me, Carol, and raise me a little; I can talk better so.'

Carol lifted the poor thin body as easily as a baby, and propped it up on the cushions.

'Thank you, that is better. Ah! don't take your arms away; let me feel them round me for a little. Carol, when I am buried, I want those words to be put on the stone. My father will let it be so, I know, if I wish it; I shall ask him the last thing. But you must remind him.'

'Oh! Tim, I can't bear to hear you talk so. You mustn't die; we all want you so much.'

'Don't cry, Carol; you will do as I wish, won't you? And, Carol, tell her how I tried to make things happy for her and you; I want her to think kindly of me too.'

He laid his head on his friend's breast and closed his eyes; the effort of talking so much had tired him. Carol thought he was asleep, and dared not move for fear of waking him; but by and by he said, 'Do you remember, Carol? I lay on this sofa when you first came to see me after the accident. I had been dreaming of you without knowing it; I thought you were an angel. And then I turned and saw you standing there in the doorway. You kissed me that day, Carol. Will you kiss me now?'

Carol bowed his head without a word and kissed him. And thus their friendship was sealed at either end.

'Father,' said Tim, after a little, 'are you there?'

'Yes, my boy.' He had come in, and was standing a little apart in the deepening twilight, humbly watching the friends. How unlike the proud man who had so bitterly resented his little son's preferring another to himself!

'Will you come here, father? I cannot see you there.' He came round the sofa, and Tim held out his hand to him. 'You and Carol must love one another,' he said, looking from one to the other, 'for my sake.' Silently the two men clasped hands over the couch.

'You must leave us now, Carol dear,' Tim went on; 'I must be alone with my father.'

Carol longed to say something, but could not; he went out without a word. Tim watched him walk away with eyes that knew they were taking their last look. Then a satisfied smile lit up his face as he turned it to his father.

THE END

Books published by Mondial

French Classics:

1. Rougon-Macquart Series:

Emile Zola: The Fortune of the Rougons
ISBN 1595690107 / 9781595690104

Emile Zola: The Fat and the Thin (The Belly of Paris)
ISBN 1595690522 / 9781595690524

Emile Zola: Abbe Mouret's Transgression
(The Sin of the Abbé Mouret) ISBN 1595690506 / 9781595690500

Emile Zola: The Dream. ISBN 1595690492 / 9781595690494

Emile Zola: A Love Episode (A Page of Love)
ISBN 1595690271 / 9781595690272

Emile Zola: The Conquest of Plassans
ISBN 1595690484 / 9781595690487

Emile Zola: The Joy of Life (Zest for Life)
ISBN 1595690476 / ISBN 9781595690470

Emile Zola: Doctor Pascal. ISBN 1595690514 / 9781595690517

Emile Zola: His Excellency (His Excellency, Eugène Rougon)
ISBN 1595690557 / 9781595690555

Emile Zola: Money. ISBN 9781595690630

Emile Zola: Piping Hot! (Pot Bouille). *Illustrated Edition.*
ISBN 9781595691231

Emile Zola: The Soil (The Earth). ISBN 9781595690883

Emile Zola: The Downfall (La Debacle). ISBN 9781595691118

2. Other French Literature:

Emile Zola: The Mysteries of Marseille. ISBN 9781595690913

Emile Zola: The Flood. ISBN 9781595690944

Emile Zola: Death. ISBN 9781595690937

Emile Zola: Fruitfulness ISBN 1595690182 / 9781595690180

Emile Zola: For a Night of Love. ISBN 9781595691217

Emile Zola: The Fête in Coqueville
(The Coqueville Spree) ISBN 9781595690869

Emile Zola: Jean Gourdon's Four Days. ISBN 9781595691224

Victor Hugo: Ninety-Three. ISBN 9781595690920

Victor Hugo: Bug-Jargal. ISBN 9781595690951

Victor Hugo: The Man Who Laughs (By Order of the King)
ISBN 1595690131 / 9781595690135

Victor Hugo: History of a Crime. ISBN 1595690204 / 9781595690203

Voltaire: The Princess of Babylon. ISBN 9781595690999

Honoré de Balzac: Ursula (Ursule Mirouet)
ISBN 1595690530 / 9781595690531

Honoré de Balzac: Maitre Cornelius. ISBN 9781595690173

Anatole France: Penguin Island. ISBN 1595690298 / 9781595690296

Anatole France: The Crime of Sylvestre Bonnard
ISBN 9781595690593

Anatole France: The Gods are Athirst (Les Dieux ont soif)
ISBN 9781595690128

Gustave Flaubert: Salammbo (Salambo)
ISBN 1595690352 / 9781595690357

Romain Rolland: Pierre and Luce . ISBN 9781595690609

Jules Verne: An Antarctic Mystery (The Sphinx of the Ice Fields)
ISBN 1595690549 / 9781595690548

André Gide: Strait is the Gate. (La Porte étroite) ISBN 9781595690623

André Gide: Prometheus Illbound. ISBN 9781595690807

André Gide: Recollections of Oscar Wilde. ISBN 9781595690814

Alphonse Daudet:
Little What's-His-Name (aka Little Good-for-Nothing)
(Le Petit Chose. French Classics) ISBN 9781595691057

German Classics:

Heinrich Heine: Germany. A Winter Tale (Deutschland. Ein Wintermärchen.) Bilingual Edition. ISBN 9781595690715

Heinrich Heine: The Rabbi of Bacharach
(German Classics) ISBN 9781595691002

Heinrich Heine: Florentine Nights.
(German Classics) ISBN 9781595691019

Heinrich Heine: From the Memoirs of Herr von Schnabelewopski
(German Classics) ISBN 9781595691026

Bernhard Kellermann: God's Beloved (Illustrated)
(German Classics) ISBN 9781595691262

Gotthold Ephraim Lessing: Minna von Barnhelm or The Soldier's
Fortune (German Classics) . ISBN: 9781595691248

Johann Wolfgang von Goethe: The Sorrows of Young Werther
ISBN 159569045X / 9781595690456

Theodor Storm: The Rider of the White Horse
(The Dikegrave; aka The Dykemaster) ISBN 9781595690746

Heinrich von Kleist: Michael Kohlhaas
(A Tale from an Old Chronicle) ISBN 9781595690760

Gottfried Keller: A Village Romeo and Juliet
(Swiss-German Classics) ISBN 9781595690791

Gottfried Keller: Ursula (Swiss-German Classics).
ISBN 9781595690838

Gottfried Keller: The Governor of Greifensee
(Swiss-German Classics) ISBN 9781595690845

Wilhelm Raabe: The Hunger Pastor
(German Classics) ISBN 9781595690753

Theodor Storm, Adelbert von Chamisso, Adalbert Stifter: Famous German Novellas of the 19ᵗʰ Century (Immensee. Peter Schlemihl. Brigitta.) ISBN 159569014X / 9781595690142

Franz Grillparzer: The Poor Musician. (Austrian Classics) ISBN 9781595691095

Marie von Ebner-Eschenbach: Krambambuli. The District Doctor (Two Novellas. Austrian Classics). ISBN 9781595691040

E. T. A. Hoffmann: The Sandman. The Elementary Spirit (Two Tales. German Classics). ISBN 9781595691170

Wilhelm Hauff: The Cold Heart. Nose, the Dwarf (Two Tales. German Classics). ISBN 9781595691187

Danish Classics:

Martin Andersen Nexo: Pelle the Conqueror (Complete Edition: Boyhood. Apprenticeship. The Great Struggle. Daybreak.) ISBN 159569028X / 9781595690289

Martin Andersen Nexo: Ditte Everywoman (Complete Edition: Girl Alive. Daughter of Man. Towards the Stars.) ISBN 9781595690333

Italian Classics:

Gabriele D'Annunzio: The Child of Pleasure. ISBN 9781595690581

Luigi Pirandello: Signora Speranza. ISBN 9781595691088:

African Literature:

Malama Katulwende: Bitterness (An African Novel from Zambia) ISBN 159569031X / 9781595690319

British Classics:

Oscar Wilde: The Critic as Artist. Upon the Importance of Doing Nothing and Discussing Everything. ISBN 9781595690821

H. G. Wells: Tales of Space and Time. ISBN 9781595691220

Oscar Wilde, Anonymous: Teleny or The Reverse of the Medal (Gay erotic classic) ISBN 1595690360 / 9781595690364

Agatha Christie: Two Novels (The Mysterious Affair at Styles. The Secret Adversary.) ISBN 1595690417 / 9781595690418

Jerome K. Jerome: Idle Thoughts of an Idle Fellow ISBN 1595690247 / 9781595690241

Virgina Woolf: Jacob's Room. ISBN 9781595691149

Jane Austen: Persuasion. Northanger Abbey (Two Novels) ISBN: 9781595691156

William Somerset Maugham: The Trembling of a Leaf ISBN 9781595691194

Howard Overing Sturgis: All That Was Possible. ISBN 9781595691293

Howard Overing Sturgis: Belchamber. ISBN 9781595691316

Rudyard Kipling: Ghost Stories. ISBN 9781595691323

US-American Literature:

Jack London: War of the Classes. Revolution. The Shrinkage of the Planet. ISBN 1595690409 / 9781595690401

Jack London: Before Adam. Children of the Frost. ISBN 1595690395 / 9781595690395

Jack London: The Iron Heel. ISBN 1595690379 / 9781595690371

Jack London: Burning Daylight. ISBN 9781595691064

Donald Windham: Two People (Gay Classics). ISBN 9781595691033

Susan Coolidge: Clover. ISBN 1595690263 / 9781595690265

Gertrude Stein: Three Lives (With an Introduction by Carl Van Vechten). ISBN 1595690425 / 9781595690425

Sinclair Lewis: The Trail of the Hawk. ISBN 9781595691132

Carl Van Vechten: Firecrackers.
A Realistic Novel. ISBN 9781595690685

Bruce Kellner: Winter Ridge (A Love Story)
ISBN 9781595690692

Gay Classics:

Oscar Wilde, Anonymous: Teleny or The Reverse of the Medal
(Gay erotic classic) ISBN 1595690360 / 9781595690364

Donald Windham: Two People (Gay Classics).
ISBN 9781595691033

Howard Overing Sturgis: Belchamber. ISBN 9781595691316

Contemporary Literature:

Bruce Kellner: Winter Ridge. A Love Story. ISBN 9781595690692

Malama Katulwende: Bitterness (An African Novel from Zambia)
ISBN 159569031X / 9781595690319

Other Books:

Frederick (Friedrich) Engels: Socialism: Utopian and Scientific
(Appendix: The Mark; Preface by Karl Marx)
ISBN 1595690468 / 9781595690463

Karl Marx: The Eighteenth Brumaire of Louis Bonaparte.
ISBN 1595690239 / 9781595690234

Frederick (Friedrich) Engels: Feuerbach — The Roots of the Socialist
Philosophy. **Karl Marx:** Theses on Feuerbach
ISBN 9781595691286

Sigmund Freud: Dream Psychology (Psychoanalysis for Beginners)
ISBN 9781595690166

CPSIA information can be obtained
at www.ICGtesting.com
Printed in the USA
BVHW050835181122
652246BV00001B/82

9 781595 691309